When Love Happens

Warren C. Holloway

GOOD 2 GO PUBLISHING

WHEN LOVE HAPPENS

Written by Warren C. Holloway
Cover Design: Davida Baldwin, Odd Ball Designs
Typesetter: Mychea
ISBN: 9781947340732

Published 2021 by Good2Go Publishing
7311 W. Glass Lane • Laveen, AZ 85339
www.good2gopublishing.com
https://twitter.com/good2gobooks
G2G@good2gopublishing.com
www.facebook.com/good2gopublishing
www.instagram.com/good2gopublishing

Chapter One

"I never thought this day would come, me in a Versace wedding dress, ready to walk down the aisle," Danelle Dupri said, looking on at herself in the floor-to-ceiling mirror, with her coworker best friends. Danelle was a natural beauty, standing six foot tall, with a slim build and just the right amount of curves strategically placed, allowing her bikini body to fit perfectly in her dress. Her glowing gray eyes were just as bright as her captivating smile, adding to her suburban girl look.

"You definitely deserve this moment, Danelle. Neither of us would have expected this to be your happy ending. This is truly a fairy tale." Aubry, her maid of honor and best friend said, reflecting back to how it all came together. Two years ago, Danelle found herself working at AmeriLink, a global tech company started by two MIT grads that never seem to be present at the company, since they were able to work from their homes.

"Good morning, everyone," Danelle said, placing her things down on her desk, preparing to take a sip of her morning coffee before diving into work.

"Somebody looks like they had a good night," Aubry stated, seeing the look on Danelle's face, which matched her mood. Aubry was a five-foot-two medium-built brunette with light brown eyes that she hid behind her studious-looking glasses, giving her the naughty school teacher look. However, she was feisty and quick to express what was on her mind, no matter what, especially if something didn't sit right with her. The Italian American, born in Johnstown, Pennsylvania, found herself working at AmeriLink thanks to website advertisements, which is how she became coworker best friends with Danelle.

"My night was okay, although it could have been better if dinner would have ended with a little bling," Danelle said, sipping her coffee while cutting her eye over to Kim, her other coworker best friend.

Kim stood five foot one, with blond hair, green eyes, and dimples in her smile and her body having curves as God intended them, to lure the opposite sex. "I'm always rooting for you to get the man of your dreams and the diamond to match, but how long has this been going on with Trevor, saying it's coming? Then he has you all excited, making you think you're going to get engaged every time a holiday or birthday comes around," Kim said. Her words were the truth, making Danelle sneer a little behind her steaming cup of coffee.

"I still had a good night, with the two of us sharing intimate thoughts as well as talks of our future together."

"Minus the ring. I bet that wasn't even brought up?" Aubry said then added, "Don't worry, timing is everything, you'll get it when he's ready."

"The two of them will be pushing walkers down the aisle when he finally poses the question," Kim said, being funny and getting a laugh from one of the men over across from them in earshot of the conversation. The sudden outburst of laughter caught all of their attention and they shifted their eyes over to this guy. Their eyes now locked on him, forcing his laughter to cease. "What's so funny, fuzzy beard?" Kim asked, looking on at this tech that never seemed to say much, though his work performance was great.

"Nothing, nothing is funny. I was just checking something out on my computer," he responded, slouching into his chair as he focused back on his computer screen.

"He's weird," Aubry said before shifting her attention back to Danelle. "Love is patient. It will come to you when you're least expecting it."

"That doesn't mean she has to wait around wasting time, being led on by Trevor, with his sexy body and bedroom eyes," Kim said, being truthful and funny.

Interrupting their morning tea talk, Danelle's cell phone sounded off, getting her attention. "Excuse me, ladies. It's Trevor, my future fiancé and someday husband," Danelle said with a smile, loving the thoughts of her own words that seemed to give her comfort in the hopes that day would come sooner than later. Hearing her say this made Aubry and Kim roll their eyes, knowing Trevor was dragging her along, but he was good-looking and physically fit, standing six foot three, with a close-shaven beard lined up to razor perfection, sparkling white teeth, a model's smile, light gray eyes, and hair cut close but combed back, adding to his flare. He also owned a local construction company, and Danelle and her girlfriends all viewed as him having the total package.

"Hello, beautiful," Trevor said, making her feel good hearing his sexy, soothing voice.

"Hi, babe, did I forget something at the house?" she asked, wondering why he had called when she just left home.

"No, no, I'm calling to let you know I have to go out of town for a day or two to close on this new contract, which will bring in more money for us," he responded, coming to a pause before adding. "Would you like me to stop by your job before I leave?"

She wanted to say yes, but the other part of her didn't want to seem clingy. She had spent the entire weekend with him. "I think I have a good image of you from this morning and the weekend," she responded with a smile on her heart and face. Aubry and Kim sat there looking on at her shaking their heads, knowing how Trevor had her in his web of love, making her sprung off his goods.

"Be good while I'm away. I'll call you when I get to where I'm going, and you can call me whenever you like, even FaceTime me before you go to sleep."

Danelle was loving the thought of seeing his face before bed, that and his sexy body to tuck her in. "Be safe. I'll talk to you later," she responded before hanging up."

"He got you, twisted, girl. You light up hearing his voice," Kim said.

"He's a good man who has it all, including my heart, plus my daughter loves him, and he's good with her," Danelle responded, smiling at the thought of her, Trevor, and her daughter Melanie being one happy family. Twelve-year-old Melanie was the light of Danelle's life. Her innocent baby blue eyes, she got from her father, who was no longer around, nor wished to be.

Melanie's smile was full of dimples. Danelle had her when she was twenty years old. Now a thirty-two-year-old mother, looking youthful herself, life was good with her daughter and man she was waiting to marry.

"I was just thinking seeing you light up like this. You have given him three years of your time and emotions. If he doesn't put a ring on it soon, just take his credit cards and go shopping, and buy yourself a five-carat diamond ring that will make him say, 'Yes, I do, and I will do anything for you,'" Aubry said, being blunt. This was also something she would have already done herself, if a man had her waiting.

"Don't pay her any mind, Danelle; it'll come. We're on your team no matter what, wishing you the best," Kim added before focusing in on the supervisor coming in on the floor, to give his morning speech, as if this was the sales department.

Each of the women knew how strict their boss was about play and no work, meaning there was no time for girl talk, because people around the world depended on AmeriLink and its technology. They also relied on the staff behind the scenes. AmeriLink became a global company in 2020, expanding to cell phones, computers, security devices and systems, and more. The company branded itself on the competitive edge of its technology and software that became compatible with the small microchip that made all gadgets interactive with their users, that being any human. It was far more advanced than previous compatible technology. The imbedded chip gathered Intel, adapting to the user, always knowing what they desired or needed, depending on moods and even when they needed it. Ranging from a glass of water to hydrate to doctor visits, down to eating, it would alert or verbally notify through all connected devices. All of this was made possible by a then twenty-two-year-old, James Michaels, a six-foot two MIT grad whose vision made him a multi-billionaire in the first year of the company going public.

He was an eccentric billionaire most had never seen in person or in public. He'd layered himself, hiring people to handle his day to

day business and operations, along with keeping an eye on things via computer. This allowed him to enjoy the fruits of his genius. *Forbes* magazine recently placed a picture of him from college on the cover of their latest issue, labeling him America's Wealthiest Man. That picture was from eight years ago. No one other than those in his immediate circle had seen him. No one had been able to take recent photos of him, because he didn't allow it. However, this had not stopped his growing business or stock. He was continuously coming up with new ways to advance his existing technology to stay ahead of the competition.

Chapter Two

After a long day at work, Danelle jumped in her red Toyota Camry to pick her daughter up from school. As always, she found herself drifting off with thoughts of Trevor, their future, and the big wedding she had been able to vividly see and had dreamed of since she was a little girl. The love she felt for Trevor was deep. All she wanted to do was make him happy, by giving him her all, 100 percent, nothing less, mentally, physically, and emotionally. She was fully invested in this relationship, awaiting to be rewarded, like most couples she saw in person and the movies that found their happy ending in love and marriage. Lost in her thoughts, she didn't realize she had stopped at the red light that had now turned green, until a blaring horn followed by road raged shouting, jolted her back to reality. "Wake the hell up, lady! People got places to go and things to do!" the upset driver said, passing her by. She turned her face up at the male driver before driving off, startled. Her cell phone sounded off. She didn't have to look to see who was calling, as it was synced to the car, using AmeriLink's technology.

"Your future husband is calling," the electronic female voice said, placing Danelle at ease.

"Answer call," she requested. The computer acknowledged. "Hi, babe, I see you must be missing me already?" she said, full of life, love, and excitement. He didn't respond. Silence fell on the cabin of the car as she waited on his response. Nothing. "Babe, are you there?" she asked, listening in to the call. That's when it happened.

"I miss you. I only want you," a female voice said, coming over the phone. However, she was not speaking to Danelle, but to her supposed to be future husband. She immediately pulled over to the side of the road, wanting to make sure this was what she was hearing.

"Trevor is that you on the other end?" she questioned, her voice slightly breaking in fear that he would respond, confirming the fears and thoughts that were now racing through her head.

Now on the side of the road, listening in, she could hear kissing, followed by a light giggle from the female, then Trevor's voice. "I couldn't wait to see you. I miss you too."

Right then, Danelle's body, heart, and mind became overwhelmed, as if hot, sharp knives were stabbing her flesh and heart. "Trevor! Trevor! Who the hell are you with!" she yelled, to no avail. Suddenly the call ended. Her eyes filled up, blurring her vision, as the emotion of betrayal took over. "Confirm call," she demanded the phone's computer.

"The previous incoming call came from your future husband, Trevor Johnson, telephone number—"

"That's enough. Call Trevor back now," she demanded wanting this new call to be different, wanting this call to be refreshing, not him who she heard or the female voice she heard.

"Calling your future husband, Trevor Johnson," the electronic female voice said.

The phone rang over five times before going to voicemail. "This is Trevor. I'm busy right now. Please leave a message and I'll get back to you."

"Busy my ass! Pick up the damn phone, Trevor!" she yelled out, crying, fearing that this love she had given 100 percent to had become a total failure. "Call Trevor back now!" she yelled out, not realizing this moment she was having was delaying her from picking up her daughter from school.

"Calling your future husband, Trevor Johnson."

"Stop saying that! No future husband would do what he's doing to me!" she yelled at the electronic voice as if it was a real person, not realizing it was her love for him that programmed this into the phone. The phone started ringing again before going to voicemail. This only added to her thoughts, emotions, and pain, making tears pour as she leaned over the steering wheel in pain. "Please tell me this isn't real? This can't be happening," Danelle yelled out. All of the good thoughts of Trevor and this future they were supposed to share together were all removed as the echoing of kisses backed by that female's voice replayed in her head. She raised her head up from the steering wheel thinking about her daughter, the only light in her life right now. She pulled off, driving towards the school that was a few blocks away. At the same time she started wiping her tears away so she wouldn't alarm her daughter, making her also become scared or sad. This was an adult thing, that a child should never be a part of. It didn't take long before she was pulling up in front of the school and saw her daughter standing there with a school teacher. Right then, she realized her emotional moment had consumed her, but it seemed to pass by so fast. Danelle still put on her mommy hat, smiling through her pain, greeting her daughter with love because she was her true happiness. "Hey, baby. Sorry I'm a little late. Traffic got me backed up," she said, also greeting the teacher with a smile. The teacher nodded her head as Melanie jumped into the car.

"Hi, Mom. I did good in school today, plus this cute boy that the girls like spoke to me."

"Don't pay them boys any mind. Your school work is more important. Besides, you don't need the heartache," Danelle cut her off, still venting her emotions. Melanie looked over at her mom, sensing something was wrong, since she normally would have good things to say if Melanie mentioned a boy or crush she had. She would encourage her that one day she would have a love like her and Trevor. Now all of that was out the door. Danelle didn't even know in this very moment where she would go, meaning since this was over. She would have to pack her things and leave. No more happy little family.

"Is everything okay, Mom?" Melanie asked, seeing her sad eyes.

"It will be," she responded, almost allowing her tears to take over again. However she contained them. "Are you hungry, Mel?"

"Not really. I could go for a vanilla milkshake." This was something they enjoyed doing together that placed a smile on their faces as they indulged in the sweet, frozen goodness.

Chapter Three

Close to an hour had passed by, and Danelle and Melanie sat enjoying their milkshakes and time together. Danelle was appreciating this moment that made her reflect back to how it was when she was single, just her and Melanie.

"Mom, this place makes the best milkshakes," Melanie said indulging in the sweet, frosty goodness. Danelle extended her napkin to wipe the corner of Melanie's mouth in a motherly way. Melanie looked up, smiling at her innocently.

Interrupting their mother-daughter bonding session, Danelle's cell phone started ringing, followed by the electronic voice alerting her of the incoming caller. "Incoming call from your future husband, Trevor Johnson." Her body tensed up as the emotions of the call earlier started streaming back through her body, making her heart ache all over, as slight echoing of kisses and the female's voice lingering in her mind. A part of her feared answering the call because he could be breaking it off with her officially, adding to the pain she felt. The other part of her wanted to pick up just to yell at him to express her pain.

"Ignore call, please." The ringing ceased. "Do you have homework today, Mel?"

"Not today; maybe for the weekend."

"Good, we can go home, find a movie, and spend some time together." Melanie smiled hearing this. "You can even pick the movie." Before Melanie was able to respond with her movie choice, Danelle's cell phone sounded off once more, the electronic voice acknowledging the caller, making Danelle regret programming it in like this. "I have to change that thing." Melanie's eyebrows raised hearing her mother say this, knowing she normally lit up at the sound of his voice or presence. Danelle saw her daughter's eyebrows raise and forced a smile to appease her as she took the call.

"Answer call." Trevor's smiling face appeared immediately, sending mixed messages to her. Her first instinct was to yell at him. Then she saw his face and luring eyes. To top it off, she noticed that he was at home in the kitchen, with a chef's apron on.

"Hey, beautiful, my client canceled, so I came back early to cook you and Melanie dinner. I've been here for over an hour, trying to surprise you two, but the surprise is on me, waiting on you to come home to this seafood alfredo with a fresh lobster tail that is getting cold."

Right at this moment, it all came to her. If he'd been home for over an hour, then he couldn't have been with another woman, and she might have been overreacting. Confused with love and anger, she lightly laughed at her behavior, managing a smile. "I'm on my way home now. Mel and I are just enjoying milkshakes."

"I hope it doesn't ruin your appetite for this good food I prepared?"

"We'll enjoy every bite of it, to show you we appreciate the time you took to make it," she said before ending the call.

"Are we still doing the movie thing, Mom?"

"Of course, the choice is yours, and Trevor will like it no matter what," she responded before getting up to exit. As they headed to the car, so many thoughts were running through her mind. The intelligent side was still processing the call she knew she heard with her own ears. Could it be a network error that made another phone cross hers or his? She would have to look further into this when she went back to work. The other part of her thoughts were compromised by her heart, glad that this man she was emotionally invested in was at home and not with another female. Now she could enjoy the night with her little family, being the good girlfriend and potential wife, with the love she brought to this relationship.

Chapter Four

"Mmmh, it smells good in here," Danelle said, entering the kitchen, coming over to Trevor, arms open, wanting his embrace. He obliged, closing in for a passionate hug followed by an intimate kiss. The kiss offset everything she was thinking previously before she entered the house. "I love you, Trevor. I only want you in my life. I hope I will always be enough for you."

"You are more than enough. This is why I took my time preparing this meal for my special lady and her princess," he responded, making her smile. His charm and way of diverting any trouble was smooth. "Have a seat, my love. The food awaits. I seasoned everything perfectly, with love," he added, preparing their plates and garnishing the tops of their alfredo.

"It definitely looks good, babe," she said, taking her fork, twirling it into the pasta, and getting a savory mouthful of seafood. "Mmh, this is food heaven."

"It's nice to know my time and effort is appreciated," he responded, taking a seat at the table and making sure everyone had a beverage too. He took a bite of the food, enjoying it, too, before speaking with a partially full mouth. "So, my love, how was your day?" Her eyes slightly widened at the thought of how her day had been thus far, meaning the call, what she believed she heard.

I'm not going to get into it now or should I? she was thinking. "My day was up and down with the girls at work and getting our new product out to the people, assuring them that it is better than before." She paused, taking her glass of red wine and sipping it to complement the food. "Then there was a phone call I received that threw me for an emotional whirlwind." She stopped speaking to take more of the wine in while checking his demeanor to see if there was any validity to these thoughts she was having. She had to know. She didn't want to be the woman strung along to be mentally, physically, and emotionally dropped at the end of it all. Trevor's eyes raised from his plate of pasta, chewing a mouth full, processing his thoughts as well as his response. Thus far, there were no physical telltale signs of him reacting to her statement.

"A phone call, huh? From one of your girlfriends?" he replied smoothly, taking his napkin and wiping the corner of his mouth before reaching for his glass of wine.

"I, I don't know who it was from. I mean, the call came from your phone. I think it was your voice," she said nervously, fearing confronting him.

"Sweety, I don't know anything about a phone call. What I do know is that I love this alfredo, and more importantly, I love you and Melanie," he responded, looking over at Melanie enjoying her food. Then he focused back on Danelle, giving her this look that meant there was a time and place for topics such as this, not in front of Melanie. They established this in the beginning of their relationship, to never argue in front of her. Trevor knew how he felt growing up, seeing his parents always arguing and having to choose between the two of them. That in itself was not healthy for a child. His words and look shut her down for the moment, and temporary silence fell on the room as each of them processed their thoughts while eating.

"*Lord of the Rings* is the movie I want to see," Melanie blurted out.

"That's the movie we'll watch after we freshen up," Danelle responded.

"So how was your day in school, my princess?" Trevor asked.

"Fun and educating," she responded briefly, covering her stuffed mouth.

"As least you enjoyed yourself. I did get you something nice on the way home," he said, excusing himself from the table to retrieve the gift he had purchased for her. He came back in with a jewelry box that read King's Jewelers inscribed in gold on the black box. He came over to Melanie opening it, exposing a diamond-encrusted angel, the size of a quarter, with her name inscribed at the top. The pendant was held by a white gold chain.

"Mom, this is so cute. Look at it. OMG, I love you, Trevor," Melanie said, full of excitement.

"A princess always deserves to have the finer things in life, just as her queen," he responded, locking eyes with Danelle, once again erasing all of her thoughts of that phone call. In this very moment, she flashed back to what Aubry and Kim said to her about getting engaged, how it would come. "Patience, my love, yours is soon to come," he said, taking a seat as she lit up with a smile on her heart and face, appreciating how thoughtful he was toward her daughter.

She was looking on at Melanie fondling her necklace, ready to show it off at school. "That is so beautiful, Mel. You also make it look good," she said before looking over at Trevor. "You did good thinking about family while you were away."

"You two are the best part of my life. I look forward to working hard to provide for our love and family."

Hearing his words was becoming an emotional stimulant, giving her heart the fluttering feeling of love once more. This good feeling was still parallel to the call she knew she heard. Whether it was him or not, it came from his phone. "You want to finish up here so we can shower and watch the movie together?" Danelle asked.

"I took a shower soon as I got in, then started dinner for us. I'll wait on you two to get it together. I'll set the movie up, plus the popcorn and candy," he responded, getting up and coming over and caressing Melanie's hair before kissing her on the cheek. Then he walked over to Danelle and kissed her soft lips, igniting that emotional fire of love and passion that made her feel good. “Mmmh, that alfredo mixed with the red wine on your lips definitely added to the kiss,” he said, making her smile.

“Eeew, I don’t need to hear your intimate ingredients,” Melanie said, getting up from the table and heading upstairs.

“You do love me and only me, right?” Danelle asked as Melanie vanished.

“What more do I need? You are the best thing that ever happened to me.” His response and calm brought back control over the situation and her emotions. She stood from the table, hugging him. He held her in his masculine embrace. “Now go get fresh and sexy for me while I get the popcorn and movie ready,” he said, tapping her bottom lightly, allowing her to feel the affection in his touch. She glanced over her shoulder, looking at him with intimate eyes, hoping this night ended on a good note. He blew her a kiss as she faded out of the room. Trevor waited a few minutes, to give her enough time to get undressed and into the shower, before taking his cell phone out to call his side love interest, Amber Michelle, a twenty-three-year-old Budweiser model he met six months ago after finishing up a job for a client. Amber was a five-foot-nine, white, blond with powder-blue eyes that were extremely alluring, accompanied by her pretty white teeth and smile of dimples. Her perky 36C breast that didn't need a bra sat perfect, flowing with her tight body and flat stomach with a diamond navel ring he purchased for her. Amber always dressed like she was going to a modeling gig or a sexy night out with her girlfriends. She was also full of life, being bubbly and hypersexual, with an appetite for Trevor and his sexy body. She also enjoyed the gifts and time she spent with Trevor, since he had a way of making her feel like the only woman in the world when he was around. Amber was a handful, too, always wanting her way, which was why she dialed up Danelle. She hoped Danelle would hear the two, so she would leave, allowing Trevor to be all hers. Trevor was made aware of the call once it ended. AmeriLink phones announce the call ending. This sent a wave of fear through him that forced him to end his date with her. He didn't want to risk staying away for a few days with this taking place.

"Hello, bad boy," Amber said, answering the phone, already knowing who was on the other end.

"I take it you cleaned up your little mess with the wife?" she stated sarcastically.

"Everything is under control, no thanks to you. I'm calling to let you know that I'll make this weekend up to you. I want to show you all I have for you in bed and in life," he said, getting light giggles from her, filled with happiness in her heart and body. She knew she was the woman on the side; however, in her mind, she was about to replace Danelle, by any means necessary.

"I love you, Trevor, so you better keep your promise to me the next time we make plans," Amber said, almost pouting, before shifting to sensual. "Mmmh, my body wants you so bad. I can sneak into your house when she's asleep if you want me to. Damn that would be so hot," she said, being extremely risky.

Trevor was smiling at the thought and how crazy she was for even wanting to do that. A part of him was entertaining it, but not now. "It sounds erotic and exciting, but I can't let you do that. You have to just wait your time. I love you pretty girl. I gotta go."

"Don't go just yet. I'm playing with my pretty kitty since I can't have the real thing. Mmmmh, Trevor, I want you sooooo bad, mmmmmmh."

Hearing her was turning him on, making him want her close and even inside of the house when Danelle went to sleep, but he had to keep control. That would be too close, especially with how loudly Amber moaned. "You sound like you're having fun without me. I wish I could join, but I have to go. I love you. Take care."

"No, I love you and your sexy body, aaaaaaah. I wish it was all over me now," she let out before ending the call. He took a deep breath, pulling himself together before rushing to secure the popcorn and movie, knowing if he didn't have anything ready when they came back down it would draw even more suspicion, ruining what he had done for Danelle up to this point to bring her back into good graces and love.

Chapter Five

An hour into the movie, Melanie was fast asleep, snuggled up against Trevor, who was sitting in the middle of the two. Danelle looked over and saw her baby girl sleeping peacefully against the man she loved so much, and it made her heart flutter with even more affection for him. "I love you Trevor," Danelle said, kissing the side of his face.

He turned, facing her and looking into her eyes, wanting to reassure her of his love and loyalty. "I love you even more. With you I am where I want to be in love and life," he said, looking at her and then Melanie before adding, "I love our family." His words stirred the intimate pot of passion inside of her, followed by a kiss.

"Mmh, you want to end this movie night on a good note?" she asked with love in her heart and lust in her eyes.

"I'm yours whenever and wherever. I'll take the princess up to her room?" he responded, placing one more kiss on her lips. As he headed up, Danelle was looking on at him in his fatherly role carrying Melanie upstairs. Then she made her way to the bedroom. After Trevor tucked Melanie in, he entered the bedroom to see the lights dimly lit and Danelle lying gracefully across the bed with her long, smooth legs exposed, leading to the pink negligée, a treat to his eyes. Her smile backed by lustful eyes was turning him on even more with each step toward the bed. He removed his clothing with each step, revealing his six-pack, firm chest with just the right amount of hair on it that led to his tight six-pack, and his V-shaped waistline. Good genetics and hard work at construction had given him this body. Now with only his boxer shorts on, he crawled onto the bed with a smile like a kid in the candy story, ready to get his sweet fix of Danelle's love. He started at her feet, placing kisses that trailed up to her thighs, before facing the sweet spot that was pulsating yet awaiting his touch. He took in her floral fragrance and gave it a light kiss before continuing up to her belly button, her breast, her neck, then her lips.

"I'm going to make slow love to your body, so you can appreciate how much I want and desire you," he said, placing another kiss to her lips before his hands strategically assisted her out of the pink negligee, exposing her body of art and perfection. Now his kisses were trailing back down over her breast and belly, finding her place of sweet passion, his tongue sliding over her pearl, stimulating her body with pleasure as his fingers entered into play with a vibrant touch, stirring more sensation.

"Trevor, baby, baby, mmmmmmh." Her moans flowed, lost in his touch of oral magic. Her stomach was tightening as the butterflies of orgasmic sensation were bouncing around in her stomach. She was also moaning and breathing loudly. "Trevor, oooooh, baby. Mmmmmmh. Mmmmmmh." With his fingers and tongue in sync sending surging sensations through her body, her moans became more intense as she was sliding across the sheets as if to escape this euphoric feeling. His magic was making her quake. Unable to hold it back, it was reaching its peak, racing through her body, wanting to be set free. "Oooooh, baby, baby, ooooooh. Oooooh, baby, mmmmmmh." Her legs clenched together, and her free handheld his head in place, bracing for the powerful orgasmic release. "Ooooooooh, oooooh baby, baby. Mmmmmmh." Her moans shifted to heavy breathing as the powerful stream of pleasure escaped, adding intense sensation. He allowed her flow to race from her body before climbing up to her, wiping his mouth. Her eyes locked on his, still breathing heavy, still feeling sensitive and open emotionally to him and their love.

"I love you and only you. No one else gets this good loving or treat," he said, slowly entering her ready place of passion with his length and thickness.

"I know. I love you too," she said, allowing him to continue treating her body with his love and passion, slow and deep, making her want this intimate session to last forever.

Chapter Six

The morning hours came quick after a long night of intimate lovemaking. Even in her dreams, she found him. However, she abruptly awoke at the sound of Melanie's voice calling out to her. "Mom! Mom! Get up. I have to go to school!" Danelle opened her eyes quickly, glancing over at the clock that read 7:15 a.m. Melanie had to be in by 8:00 a.m., and she had to be at work by the same time. She jumped up quickly.

"Sorry, baby. Let me get a quick shower, and we'll be ready," she said, racing to the bathroom.

Melanie looked over at the sleeping Trevor, shaking her head, knowing they were up all night. She could hear them across the house. "Eew, gross," she said as the image flashed into her head accompanied by the sounds she heard. She turned, leaving the bedroom quickly and heading downstairs to prepare her mother a fried egg over a slice of toast.

It didn't take long before Danelle came downstairs, hair wet, no makeup on; her natural beauty would be enough. "Thank you for making this, Mel," she said, taking a bite while heading out the door. "You did a good job, too, Mel."

"Thank you, and you're welcome, Mom."

"Today is going to be a good day, better than yesterday, well, not last night," Danelle said, getting into the car with a smile on her face, still under Trevor's spell emotionally and mentally.

"TMI, it's bad enough I got up to use the bathroom and heard you two going at it."

Now Danelle was feeling embarrassed, as if Mel had walked in on them. "Sorry," she responded, but in her mind she was like, "Not sorry," for how good it was feeling. As she was driving down the road, each of them got message alerts on their phones. Melanie checked hers first. It was a picture of Trevor with a sad face along with a caption that read: "Home alone." Melanie started laughing. "Mom, it's Trevor sending us messages and pics." Danelle came to a stop light and quickly checked her message. The pic he sent her was more adult, of his upper body still lying in bed. The caption read: "I can't believe u left all of this without saying goodbye."

She laughed, reflecting back to the intimate night, at the same time realizing she was in such a hurry, she didn't even kiss him goodbye. "I'm sorry, sweetheart," she said in a low tone.

Melanie rolled her eyes hearing her mother being lovestruck by Trevor. "Green light, Mom. OMG, he has you twisted. You can't even drive without being sucked into his world." Melanie said with a smile before shifting her attention back to her phone, checking her Instagram, Facebook, Twitter, and what was new on TikTok.

It didn't take long before she was dropping Melanie off before rushing to work. Close to a half mile away from AmeriLink, her cell phone sounded off again. This time it was an incoming anonymous call. The electronic voice made her aware of this, which piqued her curiosity to answer the call. "Answer call, please," she requested. The phone picked up. "Hello," she said, listening in for a response. There was only light breathing into the phone. “Hello, who is it on the other end?”

“Was it good?” a female voice came over the phone, speaking in a low tone, catching Danelle off guard.

“Excuse me, do you have the right number?” Danelle asked since the number was anonymous.

“Mmmh, he’s always good to my body,” the female on the other end said, touching herself, stimulated by this sadistic moment of taunting.

Danelle’s heart started racing just as fast as her mind trying to figure out who this was on the other end. “I really think you have the wrong number.” Danelle said, not wanting anything to steal her high and happiness from last night’s intimate session.

“Aaaah, aaaah, I, I don’t have the wrong number, mmmmh,” the female taunted with a sensual moan. “I asked if he was good to your body last night as he always is to mine, mmmmh, so good, mmmh.”

The phone abruptly hung up, leaving her with the taunting moans and words that were now burning like hot knives as she flashed back to the phone call from Trevor's phone. How could anyone know that she was being intimate last night?

She even started thinking that Melanie may have tweeted about it, being childish. She would check later. She pulled into the AmeriLink parking lot with so many thoughts, all of them not good, but she wouldn't allow this to overshadow her sensual night. Her body was still feeling good from it, like a hangover. She exited the car and saw another coworker that seemed to be cutting it close too.

"I thought I was going to be the only line rolling in here late," Aubry said, walking fast, catching up to Danelle.

"I take it you had a good night, too, since you're never cutting it this close," Danelle said.

"I wish. The babysitter has the flu, so I took my son over to my mom's place. Now back to you, why are you smiling and glowing? Let me guess, Trevor's sexy-ass body holding you hostage?" Aubry said, making Danelle laugh, even though part of her thoughts were on the anonymous call.

"Yes, he has me wrapped in his web of love and passion. I also had to drop Melanie off to school."

"I wish Trevor had a twin brother that would appreciate all of this," Aubry said, being feisty.

"You will get the right man soon. Right now, the Plenty of Fish and other sites have your attention."

"Really? I do check out the intellectual sites. I can't settle down with a dummy," she responded, laughing as they entered.

AmeriLink scanned their IDs followed by the microchips in their wrist that were extra security for the company. It also allowed the employees to be synced into their devices. "Welcome to AmeriLink. Would you like your profile read today?" the automated voice said as they scanned their wrists. This feature allowed the employees to know their stress level, illnesses, or what the chip detects.

"Yes, is my body overdue to get laid?" Aubry said, being blunt and funny.

"Your physical desires as recorded have been met today," the automated voice responded to their surprise.

Danelle started looking at Aubry, wondering if she had been keeping a secret on the side, until Aubry blurted out, "Dildos don't count, you stupid computer!" She looked at Danelle. "Don't judge me. Tony don't count. I need the real thing."

Danelle couldn't help but laugh at how crazy her friend was to name her dildo. "Tony, huh? So what happens if you meet a guy named Tony? How is that going to work out? Do you change the name of your toy?"

"Two Tony's are better than one, plus it's not cheating. He'll be little Tony, and the toy will be big Tony."

Danelle started laughing uncontrollably at the sound of this, because it was crazy, and even more funny because she was serious. They headed to the elevator, when a tall Afro-American male with dark bedroom eyes and brown skin caught Aubry's attention. At the same time, he found her one-piece, black, fitted dress to be sexy, hugging her curves, which were boosted by her three-inch pumps. Her lips were glossy, with the mole on the top left side adding intrigue along with her studious looking, black wire frame Prada glasses. “He could easily be Tony number two, all day,” Aubry said.

“I didn’t think you dated outside of your race.”

“He would be the exception,” she said, seeing him coming their way.

“Why is he coming over here?”

“He could be going upstairs like we are.”

“Excuse me, ladies, I’m looking for the IT department,” he said upon his approach. Both women looked on at him, thinking he was joking since the building’s features helped make sure employees and guests never get lost upon entry. It was one of the creator’s designs for the building.

“Really?” Aubry said, knowing this guy was more into checking them out. Danelle nudged her with her elbow.

“I’m sorry if my approach offended you ladies. I’m Anthony West, CEO of Elite Class Private Jet Company. I did come over here because you caught my eye, plus I’m going upstairs to the IT department.”

"Two Tonys," Danelle said, unable to resist the pun and coincidence.

Aubry burst into laughter thinking about it. "My name is Aubry Marching. Danelle Dupri is my coworker and best friend, but she's taken, so don't have any thoughts of hooking up your friends."

"Straightforward, no filter on your thoughts? That's a plus for a guy like me. I don't need any more yes men or women in my life." Anthony, standing six foot even, was a self-made mogul worth hundreds of millions. He was a well-groomed individual with a close cut with waves all the way around, his shape-up razor-sharp and flowing with his lined full beard. His tailored black Armani suit fit snug against his in shape body. The white gold Patek Philippe watch displayed his next level of class.

"We're almost late for work, so you can talk and follow us upstairs," Aubry said, getting into the elevator and pressing the button to the tenth floor.

He was taking in Aubry's Italian beauty and her upfront attitude. It was bold but not abrasive or a turnoff. It made him want to know more about her.

"Aubry, here's my card. When you find the time, I would like to get to know you over a nice dinner and a glass of wine. Anytime would be fine for me. I'm single. I don't have anyone waiting or expecting me to be anywhere," he said, hitting all of the right first impression notes.

She took his card, glancing at the credentials as well as the number, social media info, and businesses. "I'll call you sooner than later, Mr. West. I do have a five year old son. If that is a deal breaker, then you can have your card back," Aubry said, being honest and forward.

"A child's life is never a negative. It's a plus, because it molds a woman into a mother, making her a better potential wife," he responded, making Danelle's eyes light up as she felt his words as if they were meant for her.

This is something all single mothers need to hear, so they won't devalue their worth. She was thinking, "I like you already, Mr. West."

"Call me Tony," he responded, making both of the ladies laugh, reflecting back to the two Tonys conversation. He didn't realize him saying this would forever be an inside joke between them.

"Okay, Tony, I'll call you soon as I leave work today. Just so you know, I don't sugarcoat any of my thoughts or feelings. My girls say that's why I'm single, because guys don't like blunt women."

"I see. However, it increases your value to any real man that can accept what you bring. A strong woman makes a man emotionally strong, allowing the two of them to find a love and happiness worth holding onto." As they were processing his words, the elevator door chimed, followed by the automated voice making them aware of the floor and department they were on. They both exited the elevator going their separate ways. Danelle and Aubry were both smiling now that she had found someone to give her the emotional, mental, and physical attention she deserved.

Chapter Seven

Danelle and Aubry made their way over to their workstations, where they saw Kim looking busy. "Look at Mrs. Busybody, first thing in the morning, making us look bad," Aubry said.

Kim raised her head from the computer and keypad. "I sense from the looks on your faces that you have something really good you want to tell me," Kim said, eyeing them back and forth.

"I have intimate Trevor stories. However, Aubry here just caught the interest of Anthony West."

"So, another Tony. How is this going to work out in the bedroom?" Kim said, being funny.

"How do you know he'll even make it that far? No, he will from the looks and how his words seem to run off his tongue like silk caressing my ears," Aubry responded.

Kim's eyebrows raised, never seeing her coworker girlfriends lighting up like this with smiles backed by the thoughts of true happiness.

"Kim, I can vouch for her. He is a looker. He is also outside of the scope of guys she normally falls for," Danelle said.

"What Danelle is talking about is, he's a sexy black man who is the CEO of his own private jet company."

"Sounds like fun, you venturing off into new territory. It could also be the balance you need in your bold and forward life."

"He said the same thing, about a real man being able to accept what I bring," Aubry responded, taking it all in.

"I look forward to seeing who this guy is coming into our circle," Kim said.

"He's good looking, and from the brief time we crossed paths, he seems to say the right things, that didn't seem forced or cliche," Danelle said.

"Private jet owner, huh?" Kim said, looking from Danelle to Aubry. "I guess you can take little Tony with big Tony to join the mile-high club." They all started laughing, including Mr. Fuzzy beard, but he was looking at his computer screen, not wanting to make the women feel as if he was always listening in. He probably dis, not having a life of his own other than work.

Suddenly shifting Danelle's attention, she could see the supervisor coming out of the back, accompanied by Mr. West. "Aubry, Kim, there's Tony." At first they thought Danelle was joking around, until she pointed in his direction.

"He is good looking, Aubry, and put together in that suit that you probably can't wait to get him out of," Kim said, messing with Aubry.

"We haven't even gone on the first date yet," Aubry responded, looking across the room. "What is he doing with our boss? I'm intrigued to know."

The supervisor was now pointing across the room over to where the other employees were. Mr. West calmly made his way over, coming up to Fuzzy Beard and tapping him on the shoulder. He looked up at Mr. West as if he'd seen a ghost or was about to get fired. This was his life; that could never happen. He nervously gathered his things, until Mr. West directed him to put them back down and follow him. He closed his laptop before pushing his glasses up on his nose with his index finger. Then he glanced over at Danelle, Kim, and Aubry before following Mr. West to the back.

"The mystery begins, ladies," Danelle said, curious to know what that talk was about, since he, like a few other nerdy techs, never spoke to anyone other than head nods, because they were so focused on doing and being their best.

"Aubry, it's up to you to find out what's going on when he comes back. We want to know what your future one-night stand was saying to him," Kim said, being sarcastic.

"A one-night stand, Kim? I want his chocolate to melt over me every day, if it is as sweet as they say about the black man," Aubry responded.

Within minutes they were coming back out from the back. Mr. West, seeming slightly upset, was walking fast to exit, before his eyes veered off, catching Aubry staring at him with concern. "Everything is going to be okay," he said as he passed, speaking to Aubry before making his way to the elevator. This added even more intrigue. They wanted to know what took place back there. Fuzzy Beard came back to his station and sat down, opening his laptop before looking over at the ladies and giving them a brief wave.

"Oh my, I didn't see that coming," Danelle said, waving back along with Aubry and Kim.

"It's your time to shine, Aubry. Go in for the kill," Kim said, wanting answers too. Aubry looked on at Danelle, who nodded her head, because she too wanted to know what do Mr. West and Fuzzy Beard had in common, or why he was so upset when leaving.

"While I'm doing this, make sure my computer doesn't overload with assignments that need my immediate attention," she said, making her way over to the man they called Fuzzy Beard because they never took the time to get to know him or even ask him his name. The only thing they knew was he got a lot of awards for outstanding performances and breaking company records. "Excuse me, Fuzzy, I mean Mr. . . ." she said, fumbling her words. A rare thing. He looked up, seeing this beautiful female standing before him up close and personal. Normally they would pay him no mind, and simply walk past him.

"I'm sorry, is something wrong?" he asked nervously, staring at her beauty, breasts, and body.

"No, no, nothing is wrong. I'm sorry, what's your name? We've been working here all of this time, and my girlfriends and I never took the time to get to know you or the people around us," she said.

A slight chuckle followed by a childish grin came across his face. Finally, someone other than the bosses were noticing him. "My name is Jay, like the letter J," he responded, pressing his glasses back up his face with his finger.

"So, Jay, do you know Mr. West?"

"Do, do I know Mr. West? Yeah, he didn't seem too happy to be here today. Then he ran out in a hurry. I don't know why, but he figured I needed to get back to work here, so he stormed out. I don't know why; I really don't," he responded.

Aubry leaned in closer, puckering her lips, trying to lure him in to tell her what she really wanted to know, since she wasn't buying Jay's response.

"Uh oh, licky, licky lips," Jay said, followed by a chuckle of excitement.

Aubry almost burst into laughter, hearing him not only speak, but what his reaction was to her trying to seduce answers out of him. "Do you have a girlfriend, Jay?"

"I'm too busy with work, and more work. AmeriLink depends on good performances like yours, Danelle's, and Kim's." Aubry, hearing him say their names were shocked. At least he was aware of his surroundings, she was thinking.

"So, I take that as a no? I'm trying to get to the point of who Mr. West is to you and why he was here?"

"You're pretty straightforward. Yeah, you're the type that always gets what you want, huh? It must be nice. Yeah, is it nice to get your way, Aubry?" he asked, flipping it back to her.

"I guess you're not going to tell me what I want to know," she said, removing her ass from his desk. He immediately started wiping it off with hand sanitizer before organizing the disheveled papers she had moved around. He glanced over to their area, seeing that she was back with her crew, and they were all staring back at him.

"Fuzzy Beard got the best of you, huh?" Kim said.

"His name is Jay like the letter J, he said. Plus, he knows all of our names."

"Stalker," Kim added.

"I don't think he's a stalker. He's just more aware of his work surroundings than we are," Danelle responded, being the kind one. "Anyway, when you call pretty boy tonight, find out why he really was here today."

"Good idea. Now let's get back to work before the boss comes back out pissed at the lack of computer activity over here," Aubry said, taking a seat and focusing on her work in between thinking about Mr. West.

Chapter Eight

12:01 p.m.

Danelle along with her coworker girlfriends were all down in the large break room outfitted with a mini food court, that allowed all of the employees to stay close on the property, instead of going out for lunch. The ladies were sitting at the table enjoying the food they'd ordered. Danelle was eating shrimp fried rice with shrimp spring rolls she was dipping in the duck sauce. Aubry settled for a salad and slice of pepperoni pizza, with a Coke on the side to chase it all down. Kim was eating a grilled chicken salad with Asian sauce and a bottle of Dasani water. Kim's cell phone sounded off, making her aware that she had an incoming message. She wiped her mouth before checking the message. She opened it and saw a Budweiser model. She took notice to the large poster in the background with the same female. What caught her eye was the caption that read: "From a friend of a friend, for your friend."

"I don't know who sent this, but they're crazy. I don't even drink Budweiser. I like Corona and lime," Kim said smiling.

At the same time, Aubry's and Danelle's cell phones were also chiming for incoming messages. Each of them accessed their messages and noticed it was the same girl but with different posters in the background. The caption on Aubry's picture read: "You Know a Good Time When You See It."

"I hope this is a joke because I don't do women. Nothing against those who do, but it's not the life I live or look forward to. Plus, I like shots of tequila, not beer."

Danelle's message read: "We Do Have More Fun."

"What the hell is all of this?" Danelle questioned, flashing back the calls. At the same time these thoughts were airing her emotions.

"Danelle, what's going on?" Aubry asked, seeing the lone tear sliding down her face, a tear Danelle didn't realize had escaped. This made her friends concerned.

"I'm fine. What are you talking about?" Danelle responded, laughing it off.

"That tear isn't because you're happy to see Blondie," Aubry said.

"Do you know who she is, Danelle?" Kim asked, having a feeling there was more to it than Danelle was telling them.

"I don't think I do. I mean, I've never seen her before," she responded, looking down at the caption.

"Either this is a promotion, or she thinks she knows us. Either way, I don't like how it makes you feel," Kim said.

"Danelle, I want to know what the tear is all about. You know you can talk to us about anything," Aubry said, placing her hand on Danelle's. Right then her sad eyes started filling up as she reflected back to the call yesterday backed by the one this morning and now this. Infidelity was one thing, but taunting her about her cheating man, not good.

"Did he hurt you?" Kim asked, thinking Trevor had become physically abusive.

"No, he would never put his hands on me," Danelle said before taking a drink of her Pepsi. Then she added, "Okay, okay, here's what has taken place over the last twenty-four hours." Danelle went into detail about the calls up until this message and pic, as well as how it played on her mind but was overshadowed by how dinner and her night ended.

"We need to track down and confront Blondie to see if she has a problem with you, or if she's doing your man on the side," Aubry said, having Danelle's best interest at heart.

"We can track her pictures through social media. Also, when you go home tonight, confront him with the picture, and check his reaction to see if he knows who she is," Kim said, wishing she could be there to see his telltale signs of being caught.

"In the meantime, Kim and I will do our part to figure out who she really is, if she is chasing behind Trevor's sexy ass, or just crazy," Aubry stated. The ladies were not even paying attention to their surroundings or other employees listening in on their conversation—even the supervisor close by eating lunch. They finished up before heading back to work, with so much to do, as well as making sure their best friend didn't get her heart broken or get deceived by a love that didn't exist.

Chapter Nine

12:51 p.m.

On the other side of town, Trevor was overseeing a construction job with his men laying the foundation down for this new townhouse complex. Business was going well. He was focused on keeping Danelle smiling inside and out. He also knew that no matter how exciting Amber was, if he truly wanted to settle down with Danelle, then there could be no more Amber. As these thoughts were entering his mind, his foreman came over, getting his attention. "Aye, boss!" he yelled out. Trevor looked in his direction. "I think you need to go over to your truck. There is a young lady looking pretty hands on and frisky, if you know what I mean?" the foreman said, looking back over at Trevor's truck before going back to work. Trevor headed over to the Ford F-350 with the king cab and lightly tinted windows. As he closed in on his truck, he could see someone inside moving around. He came up and placed his clipboard on the hood of the truck, before opening the passenger door, only to see Amber Michelle in the cab, with a pink silk scarf around her neck, matching her pink six-inch pumps.

"Surprise, baby," she said bubbly, backed with lust in her eyes, while licking her lips salaciously.

"You're joking right?" he asked, wanting to close the door on her and walk away, but knowing she was not the type to just leave; she would wait until he came back.

"How could you look at all of this and think that I'm here to joke with you?" she responded, caressing her breast while rocking her legs open, giving him a peep at her freshly waxed paradise. "You like what I did to my pretty pearl?" she asked, holding her legs open to display her clitoris piercing with a diamond sparkle. A part of him felt weak for her exotic and adventurous side. The other part, wanted to hold onto Danelle and do right by her.

"I want you to make me cum, inside of the truck, since we never did it in here, especially with all of these people working hard," she added, sliding her hand down to her pearl. "My pretty kitty is purring for your touch. Mmmh I want you so bad," she said in a sensual, seductive tone, licking her lips and getting a rush out of her own actions.

"Amber, as much as I love and enjoy your body and your life of excitement that comes with it, we have to bring this to—" Before he could finish his words, she leaned forward and took his hand, pulling him close, placing his thick fingers into her already turned on, wet, heated body. He without question melted into the moment, not even resisting the feeling of her body at his fingertips. He climbed into the truck, fingers still in motion.

"Mmmmmmh, I miss your touch, baby," she let out, assisting him out of his pants, his pulsating thickness now in her hand. "I want you inside of me, baby. Make me feel good like you do her," she said, sounding sexual and crazy at the same time. It didn't stop him. He thrust into her body, giving her what she was craving, slamming deep, hard and fast, just the way she liked it. "Ooooh God, Oooooh God, oooooooh baby. Oooooooh, harder baby." He obliged. Hearing her intense erotic moans, he went deeper, harder, and faster. "Oooooh God, oooooooh God, aaaaah, aaaaah, aaaaah." His fast, deep and hard pace was making her body react with intense sensation matching his motions. Her legs were up as he was taking control. His breathing was picking up, feeling his body also reacting, ready to erupt with each deep stroke. His lips were up against her ear, taking deep strokes, feeling the sensation racing through his body that had reached its peak, ready to erupt. His lips against her ear followed by his heavy breathing and movement were making her release with overwhelming flow from the intense pleasure. "Ooooh God, oooooh God, it feels so good, baby. Oooooh, ooooh." This quickie came to an end as his motion stopped. Amber was appeased for now, getting her way. "I love you, Trevor. I love when you make my body feel like this."

Her words, backed by the look in her eyes, made him realize she wasn't going anywhere anytime soon. So breaking it off with her wasn't going to be as easy as he originally thought. "I can't lie, I love your body, looks, and spontaneous sex, but this sinful thing we have going on shouldn't exist, as much as we both enjoy it."

"So you want to walk away from all of this?" she said, making her body contract on his love stick. "Mmmh, I don't know what I would do if I couldn't have this anymore. Ooooh, baby, you make me moan and my kitty meow," she said, making him laugh.

He leaned in and kissed her lips, caught in the moment, weakened by her physical and visual presence. "I love you too, Amber," he said, looking into her eyes, which were glowing from his words.

A light giggle came from her feeling his affection. "You want me to turn over, so you can get it from behind as I watch all of your hard working men?" she said with a naughty look in her eyes.

"As much as I want to say yes, we can't. This job has to be done with me being hands on," he responded, removing himself and pulling his pants up. "I'll call you later, Amber."

"For more of this sexual fun or to talk," she responded, caressing her body, "about what you really want from me and this thing we have?" He reached into the back and handed her the clothes she tossed back there. "You already know what I want from you. Your time, flesh, heart, mind, I want it all with you. In exchange, I'll let my body be your adult playground."

She responded with loving and lustful eyes, charmed by him in every way. He leaned over, kissing her flat stomach before allowing his kisses to find her lips, making her smile, inside and out.

"You already have all of me," he stated, giving into her.

"I will when we're living together and Danelle and her daughter are no longer in the picture," she responded, wanting to secure her place in his life. Another reason why she sent Danelle and her friends the pictures of her modeling.

"Everything is going to be as you wish, my love, trust me. Trust that I will make all of your dreams come true," he said, placing another kiss to her soft lips, so sweet, so intimate, feeling the affection. "Now I really have to go before my guys come looking for me and find us here like this."

"We do look good together, Trevor, so imagine what our babies would look like," she said, leaving him with that thought as she walked away. His eyes were checking out her fit body with curves that were placed just right. Her words of having babies started to permeate deep into his mind, realizing all of the unprotected sex they'd been having. Was she pregnant now? he wondered. Why would she say that to me? Now he was facing that reality as if the child was here or coming soon. He would never be able to lie or explain his way out of this to Danelle.

Chapter Ten

3:44 p.m.

Danelle was driving home with Melanie in the car. Each of them was talking about their day. "I hope Trevor is making dinner again, Mom."

"Me too. If not, I'll cook something," Danelle said, then directed a phone to call Trevor. "Call Trevor." The automated voice placed the call.

"Hello, my love. How's your day going so far?" Trevor asked.

"It's hard to tell with all that is going on at work," she responded. He could sense there was something to it. "Did you make dinner for me and Melanie?"

"I just got out of the shower. It was a long day for me on this new project," he replied. The only project he worked on hard was Amber. "We could do Door Dash if you like?"

"Okay. Melanie, what do you want to eat?"

"Pizza will do for me while I'm doing my homework," Melanie responded, never looking up, focusing on posting tweets and Instagram pics.

"Anything else for my ladies?" he asked, making the two of them smile.

"A man who loves me as much as I love him, plus a ring on this empty hand."

"When he's ready, Mom. Don't rush him or you'll push him away," Melanie said, tossing her thoughts into the conversation. Danelle shoved Melanie lightly, feeling embarrassed.

"Melanie is right; it will come sooner than you expect. Besides, you already have the best part of me. I don't think a ring can do the things I can, the way you like."

"Okay, enough of that. We have young ears present."

"You should have thought about that last night, Mom," Melanie said with a smirk on her face.

"Trevor, babe, we're a few minutes away from the house. See you then."

Within minutes they pulled up to the house. Trevor came to the door just as the car turned off. He could see his two favorite ladies exiting as he stood in his black silk pajamas, with the top unbuttoned, partially giving Danelle a glimpse of his chest. "You beautiful ladies are just in time for the pizza party. I have sodas for the princess and adult beverages for my queen," he said, giving Melanie a kiss on the cheek, then kissing Danelle.

"I hope this pizza party ends like last night's dinner and movie," Danelle said, coming into the house yet awaiting the moment to blitz him with the pictures that were sent to her and her girlfriends' phones, since she now had them all on her phone.

"You two are way too much right now. I'll be down for pizza after I shower, Mom," Mel said, running up the stairs, leaving be adults to themselves.

"Danelle, do you love me and only me the way I love you?" Trevor asked, throwing her for a mental and emotional whirlwind, mind fucking her, because he was just that good, to make her feel as if he had the trust issues and she was the one doing the relationship wrong. It was to the point he even believed the lies he told Amber. It was as if he got turned on by his level of deception.

"Of course, I love only you. My mind, heart, and body are yours. I don't need anything or anyone else but you," she responded kissing his lips, not realizing this was stroking his ego.

"I have something special for my queen," he said, taking her hand, leading her toward the family room, over to the couch, where the pizzas were. "I didn't want you to feel left out from last night, when I got Melanie a gift. However, my gift to you is my love and presence," he said, reaching down by the pizza boxes to retrieve the black leather gift box that read Bello's Jewelers. He opened it, revealing a white gold Movado watch with a black pearl face. "Timing is everything. This love thing we share is timeless," he said, being smooth and calm and luring her into his world of lies and deception. He placed the watch on her wrist, followed by a passionate kiss.

"Thank you, babe. It looks nice too," she responded, happy but wishing it was a ring. His gift, without question, shifted her attention from the pictures. They sat back enjoying the pizza and wine. Melanie came down twenty minutes later. Seeing the two of them snuggled together with googly eyes in between eating and drinking, she took her pizza to her room.

Interrupting their pizza and wine time, Danelle's cell phone chimed as a message came in. She saw that it was Aubry. She tapped the screen to view the message as Trevor started pouring shots of Patron, now shifting from the wine.

The message read: "Did you ask him yet???"

Right then, it all came back to her, what she needed to do, instead of allowing her emotions and his presence to sidetrack her. She responded to the message. "No. Got distracted."

Trevor handed her a shot, and she downed it, closing her eyes, thinking about how she was going to approach this picture thing. At the same time, another message came in. This time she could see that it was Kim. It read: "Really?????? WTF!!"

Danelle quickly responded. "Got it! C U n the AM." She poured herself a shot, toasting with him saying, "A toast to real love, being loyal and honest."

Hearing her say this made him hesitate to take his shot, as he was trying to process where that came from. "To you, my love," he said, downing the shot and leaning in for a kiss.

She brought it to a halt, placing her hand on his chest, looking into his eyes. "I want to show you something to get your opinion, then ask a few questions," she said, accessing the pictures on her phone. She showed him the photo. "Do you know who this is?" she asked, displaying the young twenty-three-year-old Amber Michelle posing for a modeling shoot. Danelle's eyes locked on him, checking for anything that would suggest he knew her. Nothing.

"She's a model that's getting a lot of exposure on TV, Twitter, Instagram, and other notable social media outlets. She's even on the billboards on I-81 and I-83, I saw. Her face is everywhere. What's her name?" he said. The fact he was able to recognize her didn't make him give off any telltale signs of lying, because he wasn't, except for the name part. "So what did you download her picture for? Are you thinking about following her on IG or becoming a model?"

"No, someone sent this to me and my coworkers, with different captions," she said, swiping the screen showing him the other pictures and captions.

Upon seeing this, Trevor realized how young and crazy Amber was, wanting what she wanted by any means necessary. She was crossing the line; this was not good. He needed to contain and control her. "It's strange that someone would do that," he said.

"Strange is the call I received this morning asking if he was good to my body last night. It shook me up inside to think that the man I love with my all is sharing himself with someone else. An exotic blond that's a model, young and full of life," she said.

He leaned in, wanting to comfort her. "You're full of life and all of the love I'll ever need, Danelle," he said smoothly, placing his lips on hers, becoming intimate to shift the topic. His hand slid over her leg, parting them, only to press up against her pants and feel her love spot, making her moan at his touch. "I want to make love to you forever, so we can hold onto that good feeling in our hearts and bodies," he said, still massaging the outside of her pants up against her body, turning her on by his touch and words, giving her an emotional and mental euphoric rush. So caught up in his misdirection, she didn't even ask all of the questions she intended to.

"Mmmh, baby, let me go shower. I want to be fresh and sexy for you," she said, standing up, heading to the shower. Trevor let out a deep breath, feeling a sense of relief. At the same time, he got on his phone and texted Amber: "Are you out of your mind!!??"

"Only when of comes 2 U"

"I can't do it UR way anymore!!!"

"U Luv Me!"

"Not this way!"

"Y R U Mad???"

"The pics!"

"I'm URs 4ever!!!"

"It's over!!!"

"U THINK???"

Trevor hadn't realized he had gotten himself into a web of his own deception that he now had to figure a way out of. Amber was used to having all she desired, by any means necessary.

Chapter Eleven

5:58 p.m.

Over in Mechanicsburg, Pennsylvania, Aubry was settling in for the night after a hot bath and some take-out food for her and her son. Now he was fast asleep, leaving her with the chance to think about Mr. West. The images she was having of him, followed by his words and good looks, all brought a smile to her face. She dialed his number at the same time, saving it under Sexy Chocolate.

He picked up on the second ring. "Anthony West speaking. Who's calling?" he asked, not recognizing the number, yet always in business mode.

"It's me, Aubry, from this morning over at AmeriLink," she responded, sounding innocent at the same time, hoping he remembered who she was.

"Yes, the bold and beautiful brunette," he responded, making her light up with a smile.

"I'm calling because I liked what I saw and heard from you today."

"I take it luck is on my side, having you reach out to me. I like your bold personality. It keeps a man like me honest," he said being truthful. "So what's your child's name?"

"Tyler, my little bundle of joy," she said, being a proud mother.

"I take it he has molded you into this straight forward woman who doesn't waste any time that is valuable?"

"You can say he's a big part of it, even though I always like to be upfront and honest, no filter, just the truth."

"I agree one hundred percent, especially when entering into a relationship, because if you start on a lie, then that one lie may be the demise of the one love and person you want so bad."

"Being honest, I've never dated outside of my race. However, seeing you, followed by hearing your words, it allowed me to be open to the possibility, welcoming you and your words into my life."

"The pleasure is all mine. Now since we're being honest, I've never dated or been intimate with a white woman. Seeing you in that black dress lured me into wanting to know who this beautiful woman behind that smile was." His words made her want to connect with him on that mental and emotional level.

One thing at a time, Aubry, she thought. Get to know and see what his mental and emotional intellect is about, and the rest will come naturally. She was coaching herself through this, not wanting to rush or ruin a good thing. "At least we'll be sharing one first together, making what we do from this point special and unique," she stated, making him smile and appreciate her thinking.

"I look forward to many first with you. It's the only way to keep it exciting, while bonding and making memories." He paused, allowing his words to be processed and appreciated. "Keeping on with the honesty, I've been single for over a year now. My ex was more concerned with fashion, being noticed on Twitter and Instagram, posting our private trips and moments meant for just her and me. That's just not how I live," he said.

Aubry flashed back to her last relationship, with Tyler's dad, who was abusive. Leaving him made her strong in many ways. "I'm not like that either, other than texting my coworker girlfriends. As for my last relationship, it was Tyler's father. He was abusive mentally, emotionally, and physically. So I left before it was too late," she replied.

A brief quietness fell over the phone as he absorbed her words, wanting to place her into a space of comfort. "My mother said to me as a child, a real man doesn't hit a woman. A real man loves a woman. He shows his appreciation to God's best creation by holding her high and always protecting her in every way, including her heart," he responded. Hearing his words struck an emotional cord, making a tear form in the corner of her eye as she embraced every word spoken. She wished she would have met him before those hard times in her life. However, now she was welcoming him and all he brought, thanks to God and fate. "You're so sweet, Anthony.

I hope we can make something of this, meaning us crossing paths as we did," she said. She wiped the corner of her eye and thought about a new man, a new start, venturing off into a new world full of life and promise, a place of comfort she'd yearned for a while.

"I look forward to making something out of this with you, too, as well as having the honor to meet your little man Tyler," he responded, making her smile with words backed by the fact that he didn't exclude her son. "Aubry, how about dinner sometime soon? You can even bring your son, if you can't find a babysitter. I'm intrigued, wanting to know more about you, wanting to share your time and space." If they were on Zoom or video chat, he could have seen his words making her light up with a smile, thinking about a date, connecting more with him.

"How about Friday?" she responded, wanting this date to be sooner than later.

"I can do Friday. Any food preferences or allergies I need to know about, so I don't make a bad first impression?"

"I enjoy all foods, no restrictions here," she responded as if she was hungry now, but not for food, for love, affection, and a real man's attention and touch.

"I'll have a car come pick you up Friday. Until then, be good to yourself."

"I will, take care," she said, hanging up, still smiling like a teenager who had a crush. She briefly closed her eyes, seeing his face, hearing his words, as if they were next to her ear. She gave a light giggle followed by laughter as she opened her eyes. She texted Danelle and Kim a message that read: "Can't W8 2 CU in the AM #2Tonys." After sending the message, she headed up to her bedroom, jumping onto the bed in excitement, placing her pillow between her legs while taking the other pillow and holding it as if it was Mr. West himself. She closed her eyes and fell asleep.

Chapter Twelve

7:15 p.m.

Amber Michelle found herself sitting out in front of Trevor's house in her lipstick red CL550 Mercedes Benz. From the car, she could see the two of them in the living room, since the curtains were parted. Amber didn't like how the call had ended between her and Trevor. She also knew that he would be giving Danelle the attention that should be for her. Amber exited her car, making her way over to the house, ready to knock on the door, until a part of her wanted to get closer to see the two of them in the living room. "What are you doing, Trevor?" Amber said in a low tone, peeping into the window like a night stalker. "Get your hands off of my man, bitch," she added, seeing Danelle being intimate and loving toward him. Danelle was now caressing and removing his clothes. This wasn't sitting right with Amber, seeing her man being undressed. Danelle was also taking her clothes off down to her bra and panties. A part of Amber was ready to bang on the window then run away. Instead, she sent a message to Trevor's phone: "Don't hurt me like this!" His phone chimed, and he glanced over at it briefly before focusing back on Danelle, allowing his kisses to trail along her breast, then her side. Another text followed. "I hate you!!!" Then "You lied to me!!!" "You'll regret this night!!!"

Danelle heard his phone chiming back-to-back, so she brought a halt to his foreplay. "I can't get into this with your phone going off like that. Besides, who could be messaging you like that?"

Trevor was now caught in the moment, having to explain his way out of this in order to get back to being intimate. His hand was still on Danelle's leg as he reached for his cell phone. Once he accessed the messages and saw it was Amber going crazy, he quickly deleted them, before blocking her. "My foreman sent me an alert, making me aware someone stole the front end loader from the construction site. The police will handle it. Now back to the world's most intricate woman," he said, moving in between her legs with kisses up her thigh, before his lips found her love place with a kiss.

She was squirming as his fingers enter into play, pressing lightly on her pearl, stimulating it, followed by his tongue extending for a taste. "Mmmmmh, baby, mmmmmmmh, mmmmmmh, aaaaah, baby." Her moans became intense as his finger thrust into her tightness. Now going faster, he found her spot inside as his tongue found her place of pleasure on her pearl. "Aaaaah, baby, aaaaah baby, mmm-mmmh, mmmmh." Her moans permeated through the air.

At the same time, Amber stood there looking on, partially turned on and upset at the same time. This torment of feelings made her react by banging on the window hard, before running off. The loud, abrupt banging ceased all intimacy and moans, making Danelle and Trevor jump in fear that something terrible was about to happen. Trevor rushed over to the window, only to see Amber's car racing away, tires screeching. Seeing this replaced his intimate mood with fear, fear of losing it all with Danelle.

"Who the hell was that?" Danelle asked, also hearing the screeching tires.

"Whoever it is must be crazy," he responded.

"Should I call 911?"

"No, my love, I'll protect you and Melanie with my life," he said, wanting to reassure her that she was in good hands with him and their love.

Danelle was also out of the intimate state, he noticed, as she was getting dressed. "There goes my night and mood. Let's go upstairs to bed."

"I'll be up, babe. I'm going to secure all of the doors and windows, then check the alarm, to make sure we're safe and tucked in." She turned around, disappointed at how this night had turned out, especially with her body in the middle of release. The jolt of fear had halted all of that, ruining a good thing. Trevor immediately reached out to Amber, sending her a message. The level of anger and fear he was feeling at this moment assured him that this thing with Amber could no longer exist. "I AM DONE!!! Banging on the window, who does that!?? A child?"

Amber: I'm not a child! I am a woman who fell in love with an idiot!!!

Trevor: We can't do this anymore! So please stop calling and texting me!!

Amber: I'm pregnant, asshole!! So we can't stop and I won't stop until we're a family!!

Trevor's heart dropped, and his world with Danelle, as far as he could see, was bound to come to an end with Amber being pregnant. He would never be able to explain this away. No amount of kisses, good sex, or gifts would make her forgive or forget this level of pain.

Trevor: Pregnant? Really?

Amber: Yes, we're pregnant, dumbass! Found out today. Sorry to disappoint you with your happy family!!

Now being cornered by this newfound information, he tried to do a little damage control.

Trevor: You have to understand that I'm in a bind right now.

Amber: Really??? You didn't say this when you were between my legs! Don't worry, I'll take care of everything

Trevor: Don't do anything stupid

Amber: I already did, when I started messing around with you!!

"Are you coming upstairs?" Danelle called out to Trevor, who was out of her sight in another part of the downstairs area, as if he was checking the house. Even so, he stiffened up as if he was caught red handed. He quickly deleted all incoming and outgoing messages between him and Amber.

"I was checking the alarm, babe, making sure it's synced with our phones and door camera," he responded. Danelle's female instincts kicked in, eyeing him down as he made his way toward her. Thoughts of the events that had been taking place over the last few days were all playing in her mind. He came up on the step, preparing to kiss her.

"My mood for kisses and anything else intimate is done for the night," she said, turning to head up the steps. Trevor was now feeling the heat, knowing he had to bring calm and love back to this relationship.

Chapter Thirteen

The morning hours came, and Danelle dropped Melanie off at school before heading to work with thoughts of Trevor, the pictures of the model, the calls, and now last night's banging on the widow. So many blatant things were making her rethink what she had with him, or at least get to the bottom of it. Either way, if he was cheating, she was not going to stick around. It didn't take long before Danelle was rolling into work and seeing her two best friends in the middle of their morning gossip. Kim and Aubry halted their conversation, focusing on Danelle.

"So did you show and ask him about the pictures?" Kim asked.

"He only recognizes her from the billboards and adds."

"And you bought that line?" Aubry questioned, knowing something wasn't right with this picture thing or the calls she had made them aware of.

"I didn't buy anything. He doesn't know her."

"I bet my life savings she knows him," Kim responded, wanting to open Danelle's eyes to what was unfolding right before her. A part of her was still gripped by Trevor's love and promise of a better future.

"Okay, okay, ladies, I'm not naive to what's going on. I have been processing it all, especially after what happened last night."

"What happened last night?" Kim asked, becoming concerned and intrigued and the same time.

"Trevor and I were in the living room having an intimate session, when an abrupt banging came across the window, scaring the shit out of me, halting my orgasm."

Both Kim and Aubry gave off a burst of brief laughter at her description of her night, especially how it ended. "It's that crazy blond in the picture stalking your man. Which only furthers my suspicion about him sleeping with her," Aubry said.

Hearing her words only made Danelle feel the emotional pain, thinking of this ultimate betrayal. This can't be happening. I love this man more than anything, she thought. "I'll get to the bottom of this. I'll reach out to Blondie on Twitter or Instagram," Danelle said, now determined to appease her feelings and emotions.

"Now that we have that out of the way, Aubry has two Tony news," Kim said.

"He's the real deal, meaning a real man that's not just telling me what I want to hear. He speaks the truth as it was instilled into him from his parents and life experiences." Danelle smiled hearing this news, which was making Aubry smile as she was speaking. "We're going on a date this Friday. He even invited my son if I don't have a babysitter. How sweet is that?"

"Thoughtful, besides Tyler has to eat too," Danelle replied, smiling for her best friend, at the same time taking a seat at her desk and immediately noticing a few messages in the inbox. "I hope things work out with and then other Tony."

"I did mention that to him too. I told him I'll explain the inside joke to him one day."

"Don't run him off with that thing," Danelle's stated.

"I doubt he'll allow a toy to get in the way of him desiring all of this," Aubry said, running her hand down her side over her bottom. Kim and Danelle shook their heads, smiling at their friend before focusing on their work.

Danelle checked her messages, and there was one from an unknown account. The first read: "Never let them steal your joy. It's the light in you that brings happiness to those around you." Danelle looked around, thinking one of her girlfriends might have sent it, with all that was going on. She appreciated the gesture and words that were comforting with all she was enduring mentally and emotionally. The next message stood out to her. It read: "Why running around looking for jewels when you have a diamond at home???" Reading this anonymous message was uplifting to her. At the same time making her want to question Trevor even more in depth about the blond, the calls, and the banging on the window. She typed a brief message to the unknown account that read: "Thank you for your inspirational words. God is smiling on you." She added a few smiley face emojis before going back to work.

"Excuse me, ladies, I'm looking for Aubry Marching," the man in a gray uniform from Flowers by Design said, standing with a floral arrangement wrapped in red, gold, and black Versace silk, with even the rose petals having the Versace lion printed on them, adding to the flare and uniqueness.

"That's me," Aubry said with a smile, appreciating how thoughtful someone was.

"I have an arrangement as well as a formal invitation from Mr. West," he said, placing the flowers down and handing her the arrangement. "Can you sign here, please?" he asked per company policy, since most of their gifts started at $500 and up. The silk wrapped around her flowers alone was over a thousand dollars; however, Aubry didn't know this. What she did know and appreciate was how creative and beautiful they were.

"Two Tonys is putting in work early, making sure he gets his Italian fixing with you," Kim said, looking on at Aubry enjoying the flowers.

"First his poetic words and now an upscale floral arrangement. He's on track to being a good thing," Danelle said, then added. "What does the card say?"

Aubry was smelling the roses, really enjoying the fact that he thought of her. She took the card out, reading it. "I enjoyed our conversation last night. I wanted you to know that this is a gesture of my appreciation for you and your time. Both of which I look forward to valuing and having more of." A good feeling in her heart, plus her woman's instinct, was glad she was forward with him, getting his attention.

"You might not need the other Tony if he keeps up the good work like this," Kim said, feeling good for her best friend.

"He's going to want some of your goodies Friday. This is just the warm up to it," Danelle said, being funny.

"I don't think that's his main goal with me. Not that I wouldn't let him have me. It will be our first."

"First what?" Kim and Danelle both questioned simultaneously.

"He's never been with a white woman, and I told him I've never been with a black man. We were being honest going into deep conversation, that led to these very nice roses wrapped in a silk Versace scarf."

"I'm happy for you," Danelle stated.

"These flowers make me anxious for Friday now, wanting to show him my appreciation," Aubry said, eyes sparkling with happiness.

"Good things will come to you and Danelle," Kim said.

"Now we have to get you in the love boat, Kim, so you can share intimate gossip in the morning," Danelle said.

"My Mr. Right is still out there, but when he comes, I'll be all the way open to him and for him," Kim responded, making them laugh, including Fuzzy Beard and a female tech a few stations over.

"Maybe Fuzzy Beard is your Mr. Right," Aubry said. This made him laugh even more at the thought.

"You never know. He may have gifts," Kim fired back, making fun of herself as Aubry leaned in, eyes closed, smelling her roses.

"Look at her all twisted and ready to give the goods up," Kim said, playfully taunting Aubry.

"I keep little Tony charged for pleasure, but when it's time for the real thing, he'll be more than welcome to enjoy this Italian cuisine."

"One more thing, Aubry. Did you ask about their association?" Kim questioned, referring to Fuzzy Beard and Mr. West.

"I got lost in our conversation. I'll remember next time."

"Sounds like somebody we know, getting lost in Trevor's magic fingers and silk voice," Kim said. Danelle rolled her eyes playfully, giving off a brief smile before they all focused on their computers and work.

Chapter Fourteen

Friday 6:45 p.m.

Aubry was at home standing in front of the mirror, after taking a hot shower, before getting dressed, looking sexy in her light blue YSL fitted jeans that were hugging her God-given curves effortlessly, flowing down to her six-inch tan suede red bottoms. The white blouse was resting perfectly on her full perky breast, which was visually appealing. No makeup, just her natural look with a little lip gloss to make her lips kissable while enhancing her smile. "Don't mess this up, Aubry," she said, coaching herself, knowing she could be too bold at times. Aubry did manage to find a babysitter for her son. This also gave her adequate time to vet Tony before bringing him around her son. No matter how nice his first impressions were, she was still a mother protecting her baby boy. Aubry turned to the side, checking out her ass in the mirror. She wanted to see how it looked, knowing Mr. West would also be checking it out as she walked in front of him. The thought of this made her smile. Interrupting her thoughts, her cell phone chimed. She made her way over to the end of her bed where the phone was. "You better not be canceling on me," she said, seeing that it was a message from Tony.

She opened the message that read, "R U Ready 4 2nite?"

Aubry: Looking good, waiting on you.

Anthony: Ride @ 7PM

Aubry: Okay, C U then.

She grabbed her powder blue Prada clutch and made her way downstairs. At the same time, she could hear a horn out in front of her place. She opened the door, seeing a candy apple red Bentley Flying Spur, with custom features, along with a driver standing outside of the car. "Ms. Marching, I'm Marcus. I'll be your driver this evening," he said, opening the back door and allowing her to enter elegantly, looking the part of this new lifestyle she was entering into, being whisked away in the custom luxury car, with TVs in the headrest and cherry wood throughout accompanied by plush, soft, tanned leather seats, something she immediately noticed as she melted into the interior. She also noticed the square black leather box with her name engraved on it. This alone was making her heart smile as she reached for it. She caressed her name on the top before opening it and seeing the gourmet chocolates with her name on each one, in edible gold flakes. The lid of the box as she opened it all the way read inside: "Chocolate stimulates the mind, unleashing endorphins that open the heart up to being catered to. I want to be the chocolate in your life that caters to you and your every desire." Aubry's smile was not only on her face. She could feel these words as if he was presently whispering them in her ear. She took a piece of the chocolate out and took a bite. "Mmmh, this is so good," she let out, savoring the flavor that was melting over her taste buds. At the same time, she looked out the window, allowing her thoughts of a future with him to form. Lost in her thoughts, over twenty minutes passed by before the Bentley pulled up to Sweet Desires, a five-star restaurant located in Hershey, Pennsylvania, known for their infusion of gourmet chocolate in their foods.

"Enjoy your evening, Ms. Marching," the driver said, allowing the valet to open the door. She took a moment after exiting to look around at the high end luxury cars and some familiar celebrity faces.

"Welcome to Sweet Desires, Ms. Marching. Mr. West awaits you inside," the valet said. "As soon as you enter, the maître'd will take you to your table."

She made her way inside, being greeted by opulence with the decor, the lights perfectly set, low music being the backdrop, just right for conversation. "Right this way, Ms. Marching," the maître'd said. Taking one of the burgundy leather menus with gold trim, she led the way to the table, continuing to speak. "Today's creation is fresh lobster tail over a bed of sweet and spicy chocolate drizzled rice. The flavors together are explosive over your pallet," she said, looking back at Aubry with a smile. "We also have blue crab ravioli in a white chocolate sauce that'll have you feeling like you took a dose of endorphins with how it stimulates the mind and body once it hits your tongue," she said before coming to a halt and gesturing for Aubry to walk past to her table. She needed no more guidance, seeing Mr. West, now standing in his tailored light gray Sean Jean suit with platinum AW cufflinks, matching the AW buttons. His pocket square was red, flowing with the red shirt. She also noticed how well-groomed and manicured his nails were too.

"You look extremely beautiful, Aubry," he said, making his way over to her, extending his hand and taking hers to kiss. "Thank you for coming out to join me," he added, pulling out her chair.

"Thank you for the invite and chocolates. I could have eaten the whole box, but I didn't want to ruin dinner," she said, taking a seat.

"I'm glad you didn't. Then I would have been eating by myself. I don't like eating alone. That's why I'm looking forward to sharing many dinners and breakfasts with you," he tossed out there.

"Thinking ahead huh? I can scramble eggs and make a few omelets if I have to," she said, looking around. "I might not be able to do five-star like this restaurant, but I cook with love."

"This place is one of my investments, as well as a treat to you, since the food is amazing."

"Having so many investments and business ventures, will you have enough time to slow down, to make room for me in your life?" she asked, not really one for the flashy stuff if it was a distraction from the love she sought.

"My businesses don't control me; I control them. So if you're concerned about me making time for you, and even Tyler, I look forward to that one woman who can enjoy my time and success, as long as they embrace all that I bring morally, emotionally, and mentally. Can you handle that?" he said then sipped his lemon sparkling water.

She wrapped herself in his soothing words. "I can handle all that you give, as long as what you give is for me and about me," she said, winking and smiling. "Now let's eat. I want to try the lobster creation the maître'd told me about."

He gestured the staff to come over. "My name is Justin, and I'll be your server this evening. What would you like to drink?"

"Anthony, would you think less of me if I ordered a shot first, since I'm a little nervous?" Aubry asked.

"Do as you please as long as you're being you and not anyone else, I'll discover later."

"Okay, Justin, give me a double shot of Herradura tequila please."

"What will you have, sir?"

"Give me what she's having, so we can share this moment of fine tequila. When dinner comes, bring out a bottle of Laubade 1961."

"Good choice, and a great year for that wine, sir. Now for dinner, what would you two like?"

"I'll try the chef's lobster creation," Aubry said, thinking about the maître'd's description of it.

"I'll have a Kobe steak medium with the black truffles and chocolate."

The server placed their orders before returning with their drinks.

"Let's toast to a good night and a future of promising things," Anthony said, raising his shot glass, eyes locked on hers. They downed the shots, feeling the heat that's just right, not too harsh.

"I forgot how strong that is, but it takes away the nerves and starts the night," Aubry said, then added, "Not to deviate from getting to know you, but my coworker girlfriends want to know why you were talking to Fuzzy Beard then stormed out as you did? Did he get in trouble?"

He was staring at Aubry, trying to assess her true intent for being here tonight. Why this question? Was there something behind it? he wondered. "As I mentioned before, I'm an investor, so I was told something came up with one of the techs. This needed my immediate attention and presence."

"What did he do?"

"Company business. Now can we get back to the date please?" he said, not wanting to discuss business when there was a beautiful woman sitting across from him in need of his mental and emotional wealth.

Aubry, on the other hand, had her own suspicions but didn't want to ruin the date with her bold interrogation. It didn't take long before the food came looking like art. Aubry took out her phone and took a picture of it. "We normally don't allow cell phones inside here due to the celebrity clientele who pay a lot of money to be here and have their privacy."

"Don't worry, I'm not going to snap pictures of them. This is just to show my friends how pretty this food looks, plus for memories," she said, snapping the picture before putting her phone away.

"There will be plenty of memories, moments, and stories to tell them about," he said, making her feel good with him looking forward to the future. Dinner came, followed by more conversation then dessert. Vanilla bean ice cream with edible gold flakes and gold chocolate chips, with two small square pieces of cake the size of a fifty-cent piece. Elegant yet picturesque and packed with flavor.

"I can say I really enjoyed myself with you, our conversation, and this good food," Aubry said.

"Me too. You are one of a kind, which is a good thing. I want to see and know more about you. So how about I buy the groceries and you cook next time?" he said. He didn't really need her to cook. He had his own personal chef at his place, plus he could easily afford to eat out anywhere. He wanted to bond more with her, to see how she was at home.

"Just so you know, I'm not going to have a fancy car come pick you up to come to my place," she said, making him laugh and spill a little of his ice cream. She took her napkin and wiped the corner of his mouth. He took her hand and kissed it with passion.

"I have a good feeling about you, Aubry. Call it instinct. Having the world and riches means nothing if you're alone."

"No lies, no games, no secrets, and you'll never be alone, because you'll have me around to be the balance you need in your life," Aubry said.

They continued taking a little more and then went out to the Bentley. Once inside the car, they held each other, sitting close in silence as the car drove off. Her thoughts were of how wonderful this man was. He was thinking, "This woman is what I've been looking for."

In the midst of their thoughts, each of them turned to face one another and moved into a passionate kiss. It was warm and affectionate as if they'd known one another for some time or in a past life. She hadn't been kissed in over two years, and it felt new and fresh to her. For him, his lips seemed to melt into hers as their tongues intertwined, finding more passion in this kiss. "Mmmmh." She let out a light moan, being turned on by the kiss. The wine and shots she drank also enhanced this feeling. She knew she had to be a lady, but her hormones were stirring inside of her. She took hold of his hand, guiding it down to her belly before pressing his hand into her pants. Another light moan. "Mmmh." His fingers slid into her pants, guided by her hand. His heart was beating fast as he reached her close shaven kitty that was soft to the touch. Now going a little further, his long, thick fingers found her love, which was warm, and parting it, thrust his fingers into her tightness. "Aaah, aaaah, it's tight, mmmmh, aaaaah," she moaned, pulling him closer as he thrust his fingers into her body, sending pulsating waves of erotic pleasure through her heated flesh. She's was glad it was not her fingers or vibrator pleasing her body, as it had been for the last two years. "Aaaah, aaaah, you're bad, aaaaah, aaah." Lost in the moment she caught the driver looking into the mirror. She didn't feel embarrassed. She placed her lips on Tony's to muffle the moans as her body started erupting with pleasure, stimulated by a man's touch she's yearned for. His fingers were going faster, hitting her spot, sending a striking sensation surging through her body to the point she halted his magic. "Aaaah, aaaah, okay, okay, I'm done, okay. Aaaah, I'm done, aaah," she moaned as he removed his fingers and prepared to wipe them off until she said, "Get a taste of it so you know what you're going to be coming back for." Aubry looked on at him with sensual bedroom eyes, turned on by his touch. He obliged her command, savoring her flavor with a smile, intrigued and wanting more of it.

"I have to say, Ms. Marching, you have made this night more interesting, captivating my mental, emotional, and now physical attention," he said, looking on at her beauty inside and out, wanting more. He settled for a kiss right now, seeing the driver had pulled up to her place. "I look forward to our next date," he added as the driver came around, opening her door to exit.

"I'll call you in the morning, afternoon, or evening. Maybe all three times if you don't think I'm crazy?" Aubry said, laughing at her own words as she stepped out of the car.

"Either way, I'll be waiting to hear from you," he responded, watching her walk away, looking as sexy as she did when she came into the restaurant. Her ass fitting in the jeans perfectly. She added to her stride, giving him a visual show to appreciate and want to see more of. Once on her porch, she turned around and blew him a kiss before vanishing into her house to think about this romantic night.

Chapter Fifteen

Saturday morning came quick, and Aubry woke up with a smile, having traces of her date night lingering in her head. She wanted more of his time and touch. She didn't want to wait until Monday to give the gossip to her girlfriends, so she sent the same message to Kim and Danelle.

Aubry: Date night sooooo romantic. #Magic fingers.

Kim: ALREADY???

Danelle: Tell me more.

Aubry: Real gentleman, love the dinner, dessert, and the ride home. His touch, I melted on his fingertips.

Kim: You gave him your goodies already?

Aubry: No, just a taste of pleasure.

Danelle: So magic fingers nothing else??? That's a tease.

Aubry: That was it. Besides it was enough for me. It's been two years, remember? I wanted more, but I remained a lady.

Kim: Guys don't care about first night booty or waiting.

Danelle: He's the one 4 U.

Aubry: I feel the same after the deep conversation.

Kim: You ask about Fuzzy Beard?

Danelle: That wouldn't have been on my mind.

Kim: We know Trevor makes her forget about everything.

Kim's words stung a little, making Danelle resent them somewhat.

Aubry: He said it was nothing.

Kim: Don't fall in love and get all fancy on us.

Danelle: We like to travel too.

Aubry: I wouldn't trade my friends for any man.

Danelle: Aww, you're so sweet and full of it. You and the two Tonys will be traveling the world sexing it up on every continent.

Aubry: I'll still have time for you crazy ladies.

Kim: Gotta go, just finished cycling, trying to keep this body in shape, awaiting Mr. Right.

Aubry: C U Monday, Kim.

Danelle: About to spend some time with family.

Aubry: Love ya, C U Monday, hopefully with more juicy details. After they were done group texting.

Danelle, Melanie, and Trevor were preparing to go to his family's lake house. Danelle made her way to Melanie's room to see if she was ready. "Mel, did you pack what you need for the trip?" she asked, zooming in on the screen of Melanie's phone and seeing she was FaceTiming someone. "Who is that and how old is he?"

"His name is June Parker from my school. Why are you embarrassing me?" Melanie responded.

"June Parker, we're about to take a family trip, so she has to go right now. She'll call you later," Danelle said, becoming motherly and protective. Melanie rolled her eyes, not caring for her mother's actions. Danelle exited, leaving Melanie to get her things together, no matter how upset or embarrassed she was right now. Danelle made her way into the bedroom, unnoticed by Trevor, who was on the phone speaking in a low but audible tone. "This isn't how I want things to be. I'm working on it, and you have to be patient. Yes, yes, you'll have it all. Let me handle this. Me too. I'll speak with you later. Yes, I do," he responded, hanging up the phone and turning around to see Danelle standing there, furious and emotional with thoughts of everything that has taken place, and now this. Trevor was not helping, with the shocked, "I'm caught" look.

"The guys at work are messing with me, babe," he tossed out there, hoping to divert her negative thoughts.

"I didn't ask you anything. But since you're jumping to conclusions that I wanted to know who you were speaking with, I know it wasn't the guys at work, because you don't speak to them in a low, calm, sensual tone of voice." Danelle said, placing her bags down. "What's her name?" she asked, folding her arms, staring at him, not wanting to keep turning a blind eye to the obvious.

"Sweetheart, what are you talking about? That wasn't a female," he responded, walking closer to Danelle, trying to place his hands on her, to ignite his touch and charm.

However, she stepped back, shaking her head. "I want to know who she is. Is it the girl in the pictures? Or is it the crazy bitch calling my phone!"

"If you like, you can check my phone for the numbers dialed and received," he said, extending his phone to her. She didn't take it. Then to put the icing on the cake, he turned around, stepped over to the edge of the bed where his suitcase was, removed a Tiffany blue jewelry box, and opened it, revealing the two-carat solitary diamond ring. “If that was a female on the phone, you think I would be taking you to the lake house to propose to you?” he said.

Her arms still crossed, she was torn in the moment, seeing this ring that she’d been waiting years for. The other part of her woman’s instinct was telling her not to be naive, because his actions, as well as the anonymous calls and pictures, said there had to be someone else. “Okay, let me see your phone.”

“What? So, you’re going to ignore this flawless diamond ring to check my phone?”

“That diamond means nothing if the true identity of our relationship is on the other end of that phone,” she said, coming over, grabbing the phone, tapping the screen, and accessing the previous calls out and incoming. She came across a number that was saved under the title 6Pack. At first thought, a man came to her mind, but it hit her all at once, as flashes of the Budweiser model in the poster entered her mind vividly. She tapped the screen, dialing this number, before placing the phone on intercom. A part of her feared her intuition. Her heart was beating just as fast as her thoughts on how this was all about to unfold. Suddenly confirming her fears, a female voice answered the call, the same voice she recognized from the calls she received.

"Hi, baby, you miss me already?" Amber Michelle said, answering the phone.

Danelle stood silent as pain soared through her flesh like a thousand hot knives stabbing at her heart. The tears, like an unexpected thunderstorm, began to flow. Trevor looked on, wanting to explain his way out of this.

"Trevor, baby, don't be silent. My body wants you to make it purr like the other day in the truck," Amber added, unaware Trevor wasn't the one who had called her.

Danelle dropped the cell phone as she turned, leaving him to the call. "Melanie, get your things. We're leaving now!" she yelled out. Melanie immediately sensing something was wrong.

Trevor ran out of the bedroom, seeing Danelle rushing down the steps. "Danelle, it's not what you think."

"Shut the hell up, Trevor! Everything that comes out of your mouth is a lie! I don't want this anymore! I don't need this around my child!" Danelle shouted, leading Melanie down the steps with her. He followed, trying to think of the right thing to say, but there was nothing he could say or do to make this work. As she made it out to the car, he stood in the doorway watching this good thing in her flee in pain, which was brought on by his antics. Melanie seeing her mother in tears, also started feeling emotional. Melanie snatched the chain from her neck that Trevor bought and tossed it toward him. This stung deep in Trevor, knowing he hurt this innocent child in the process of his unfaithful ways.

Danelle drove down the highway for close to ten minutes before pulling off the side, to bawl in tears, filled with pain, blindsided by it all. This wasn't how her love story was supposed to end. Melanie leaned over and rested her head on her mom, wanting to comfort her. "We're going to be all right, Mom. We don't need boys to make us happy," Melanie said, wanting to make her feel better.

Close to twenty minutes passed by before Danelle pulled it together long enough to drive to a hotel, where they would stay until she figured things out. She didn't want to go to her parents because they thought highly of Trevor. This would be a total embarrassment to her, as well as a second level of emotional pain she would endure explaining it all to them. She gave him her all, heart, mind, and body. And just like that, he tossed it away. What thinking man would turn his back on a woman and a love like this? She's questioned herself over and over, as if she was to blame for his infidelity.

Chapter Sixteen

After a long emotional weekend, Danelle returned to the house early Monday to get some things for Melanie to go to school, along with things she needed. Trevor was at work. She knew this; otherwise, she would have never come, fearing running into him and his lies. Just walking into the house that used to be home, the house of love and passion, it all felt empty now. Lost to his deception and lies. Melanie gathered her things quickly, since they were already twenty minutes late. She would explain why. As they were driving to school, Danelle made her daughter aware that they would go to her parents' place, so they didn't waste money on hotels and eating out. As she was preparing to call her mother to make her aware of her unexpected stayover, an incoming call came through.

"You have an incoming call from your future husband—"

"Ignore call, change identification to the cheating son of a bitch."

"Request done."

A pause came before the electronic female voice came back over the car's intercom. "Incoming call from the cheating son of a bitch." Both Danelle and Melanie laughed through the pain and anger, hearing the automated voice announcing the call.

"Answer call."

"Danelle, baby."

"Don't call me baby. You ruined that privilege. Why did you call?"

"I want to talk to you."

"You are, and right now you're wasting precious time. Time that I could be spending with my daughter or alone finding myself without you."

"I don't want this to be over. I want us to work it out. I want Melanie to be happy too."

"Don't put me in it, especially since you hurt my mom," Melanie stated.

"I'm sorry, Melanie," he responded.

"You will be since you cheated on my mom. She'll never forgive, and neither will I," Melanie said as the car came to a stop. She opened the door. "I love you, Mom, and I'll see you later."

"I love you too, Mel," Danelle responded before driving off. "Now back to you, Trevor. There will never be an us or a you and I thing again. I gave you love, and in return, you gave me lies and deception. I can't allow you back in my life, knowing that I was sharing you with another woman."

"Danelle, please, please come back home so I can make it right," he pleaded, not realizing she had already hung up the phone.

It didn't take long before she rolled into work. As she was coming toward her workstation, she noticed Fuzzy Beard walking away from that area. Her level of curiosity was raised, especially when she noticed that Aubry wasn't here yet. Maybe she's with Mr. West? she was thinking. Kim, where is she? Neither of them had sent her a text, so she sent them one.

Danelle: No work Monday or what?

Aubry: OMG, I'm sooooo late!! On my way. Got caught up with Tonys #2Tonyphone sex.

Danelle started laughing at how crazy Aubry was. This laughter made her feel good.

Kim: Don't feel good. Save the juicy details for tomorrow, luv ya.

Danelle: Get well, luv ya 2.

Danelle made her way to her desk, seeing a Valentine's Day card propped up on her computer. Right then she put it together—Fuzzy Beard put it there. How cute, she thought. She opened the card boasting two hearts, red and silver. The outside read: "We all need someone on days like this. Happy Valentine's Day." She smiled because it was thoughtful, and the timing was right. She opened the card and read, "Love yourself first, and this day will be even more special. Happy Valentine's Day. Respectfully Jay, like the letter J." Reading this made her laugh and smile.

"Excuse me, Jay like the letter J," Danelle said, getting his attention. He turned around partially, nervous it seemed, never being one for face-to-face with his office secretly admired. "You put this card over here, right?" she said, holding it up.

"I'm sorry you don't like it. We all placed cards on the desk of people we think are nice. I'm sorry."

"Don't be. This card is nice. It actually made my morning thus far, after having a long weekend. I see you took time to pick this out."

"I'm a good listener. I know what's going on around here; not that I'm nosey, I'm just aware," he said nervously.

"A good listener huh?"

"Yeah, but not like psychologist or anything, more like paying attention to detail, so I can figure out how to make things work or enhance what already exists."

"Since my friends left me alone this morning, can I get your male opinion on something?"

He pressed his glasses back up on his face, feeling excited that his office crush was asking him over to her workspace to chat. "I, I have so much to do, and I don't want the big people to come in here yelling and pointing at us." His nerves were getting the best of him, because he was really thinking: "Hell yeah, I'm on my way."

"Don't worry, I'll talk while you're working, since you're a good listener," Danelle said, continuing on filling him in on her painful weekend as well as the calls and pictures that led up to her suspicions.

Jay stopped working and turned to her, wiping the corner of his eye, feeling the pain she was going through, especially having her daughter mixed up in this. "Oh boy, that is really sad that he lacked appreciation for a woman like you. His actions show he doesn't deserve you or the time you're willing to invest into him," Jay said, adjusting his glasses. "I'm not a preacher or nothing, but my parents used to say, there is no time like God's timing. You can decide how you wish to interpret that, but I say fate has its way of placing people strategically in life to cross paths. So don't worry; your happiness will come to you," he said, impressing Danelle, since she never took the time to speak with him as long as he'd been here.

"Thank you for allowing me to pour out my pain and giving me good feedback."

"Don't let him lure you back, because emotional and mental abuse is far greater and more lasting than some physical abuse. Neither is good or healthy. Statistics say a woman will go back up to seven times before it's too late. You need to find one man, that only sees you as one woman, so you can share one love that will outlast life itself."

Danelle was now warmed by his comforting words of wisdom that had given her new meaning and a new approach. But now she had to go through the healing and loving herself process. As she was thinking, Aubry came in, full of energy, thanks to her toy and phone conversation with Mr. West.

"Uh oh, what are Danelle and Jay like the letter J talking about?" Aubry asked, eyeing the two of them.

"Nothing, I'm working over here like you should be," Jay said, then added. "You're one hour and forty-two minutes late, with a few seconds ticking away until you punch into the clock and log onto your computer," Jay said, reminding her.

She rushed back to her computer and logged in.

"Thank you, Jay, for the card and conversation," Danelle said.

"The card was meant for you. As for the talk, we all need someone to listen to us every now and then," he said, then focused back on his work.

Danelle made her way over to Aubry, ready to break the bad news. "Before you tell me the juicy details about your night, I want to let you know, Trevor and I are officially over."

Aubry's hand raised to her heart, feeling the pain as she looked on at her girlfriend. "I bet you caught him with that beer bitch, huh?" Aubry stated, flashing back to the pictures.

"Not quite, but I walked in while he was on the phone with her."

"It's a shame you wasted your time and love on that asshole."

"He even had the nerve to pull out a Tiffany's engagement ring trying to overshadow him being caught."

"You should have taken it and sold it online or exchanged it for a ring or a bracelet to make you feel good. Another good idea, we should pour gasoline on all his clothes, set them on fire, and get drunk watching them burn," Aubry said, displaying her vindictive side.

"That would be comforting, to see his face while everything burned, but I'm not even going to give him that much attention. It's over, and I'm done with him," she said, ready to love herself past the pain he had brought on her.

Chapter Seventeen

Close to three months had passed by since the tumultuous ending of Danelle's relationship with Trevor. She hadn't looked back once, even with the threatening calls from him, promising suicide if she didn't come back. All tactics trying get her under his control. He was still living a lie, sleeping with Amber, who was now four and a half months pregnant with his baby. Danelle wasn't focus on finding love. Her mind was set on getting back on track with a little apartment she got for her and Melanie. As for Aubry, she and Mr. West were officially a thing now, keeping them updated on juicy details each morning. Kim had also found someone online but hadn't met him in person yet. No one had even seen pics of this guy yet. She wanted it to be a secret until she figured him out. All they knew was he worked out in California at another media outlet company. They continued speaking with Fuzzy Beard and even met those who worked in the office. This morning they were all talking and laughing at Fuzzy Beard with his wisdom and random comments. Their laughter ended when they were abruptly cut off by a distraught Trevor, who entered under false pretenses, since he and Danelle were no longer a thing.

"Danelle Dupri! Where are you?" he yelled out with anger, looking like he hadn't shaved in months or slept in days. The pregnant Amber wanted him when he wasn't available. Now he discovered her truth, that the baby she was having might not be his, because she was also being entertained by a married man. Karma had come back, multiplying, since Danelle no longer wished to look at him, let alone be with him. He was closing in fast, seeing them now standing and looking in his direction.

"What are you doing here, Trevor? She doesn't want you anymore!" Aubry said firmly.

"Shut up, you little bitch. This isn't about you!"

Jay, not one for being confrontational, stepped forward and extended his hand, seeing the loud and fast approaching Trevor looking to be a threat to the ladies.

"I told you I love you and only you! Why are you doing this to me? Come back home!" Trevor said, now within five feet. "Move out of the way, you nerd!" he shouted, staring at Jay with his hand still extended. As soon as Trevor's hand reached out to slap Jay's hand down. He reacted swiftly, grabbing Trevor's wrist and pulling him in fast, chopping at his throat before kicking the side of his leg behind the knee and dropping him. At the same time, he twisted his arm back, leaning in and speaking in a low yet different tone of voice that also startled Trevor, especially looking into his eyes. Right then Trevor stood, eyeing the women, before turning around to leave, ashamed and defeated, physically, mentally, and emotionally.

"OMG, Jay turned into Jason Bourne. My mind is officially blown away and impressed all at the same time," Kim said, stunned at what had taken place.

"No, no, I'm not Jason Bourne. I, I was just making sure he didn't hurt you pretty ladies. I didn't want him to hurt anyone, especially Danelle. He looked like he was coming for you. I couldn't let that happen. He won't be back. I promise you this," Jay said, pressing his glasses up on his nose, seeing that Danelle had a shocked look on her face.

"Thank you, Jay," Danelle said, suddenly wrapping her arms around him. It was the fear she was feeling of what could have taken place if he hadn't been there. Kim and Aubry also joined the hug, making him feel appreciated.

"Uh oh, group hug. This is nice," Jay said, feeling extra special.

Danelle released her hug and kissed him on the cheek. "We need more men like you around, Jay," Danelle said.

"There's only one Jay. I know how to treat people with respect," he said, making them smile.

"We need to find you a woman to be nice and respectful to, Jay," Aubry said, glancing over at Danelle.

"She's single, and ready for the world of emotional happiness."

"I'm single, too, but I know her type, and I'm not in that group."

"A good woman will find you, when the time is right, Jay. You have all the qualities needed," Danelle said with a gentle, kind smile, caressing his shoulder.

His eyes following her hand, instinctively he placed his hand on top of hers. "Thank you for seeing me in a different light, saying these good things," he said leaving his hand.

For some strange reason, she had seen past the person standing in front of her, with this fuzzy beard and somewhat greasy hair from too much gel. However, that vision came to a halt when her phone sounded off, announcing her landlord. Something must be wrong, since she paid rent three months ahead. "Hello, this is Danelle speaking."

"I'm sorry Ms. Dupri, but I have to ask you to move out immediately."

"What? Why?" she asked, her heart dropping, thinking about where she and her daughter would stay. Her facial expressions and tone of voice also alerted those around.

"This morning there was an outrageous man banging on your door, waking the neighbors. He even became physical with your neighbor before kicking your door in. We just can't have that type of behavior here. It's not safe for everyone else that lives here."

Hearing this made her feel so much pain and fear of what to do next. She was now hating Trevor for this, having caused her this pain and anguish months after their breakup. "This is not good, ladies.

Her eyes are welling up." Jay said, looking on at Danelle.

"What did he do now?" Aubry asked.

"He kicked my door in and became physical with my neighbor, so they're evicting me and my daughter immediately."

Jay, hearing this, could feel her pain, knowing how when he was a child, his father left his mother and they struggled to find a place to stay. He remembered snuggling next to her in the car, being warmed by her motherly love. "No, no, no friend of mine will ever be without a roof over their head," Jay said, walking over to his desk, opening the drawer, and taking out a set of keys before returning to the ladies.

"Danelle, please take these keys to my apartment. I don't stay there anymore because I'm so busy with work and other things."

"Hold up, Jay. It's nice, but she has a daughter, and if you plan on popping up when they're in need of privacy, it'll be a little creepy," Aubry bluntly stated.

"I'm not going to invade her space. I respect her. Besides, I know my boundaries, and it's here at work."

"Thank you so much, Jay. I promise I'll pay you back," Danelle said humbly.

"Don't worry about paying me back. This is my kind gesture to you and your daughter. I'll text you the address. Right now, we have to get back to work. There are people in the world depending on our skills and expertise," he said before walking away.

As soon as he was far enough away, Kim and Aubry started whispering to Danelle. "If he shows up in the middle of the night, use this," Kim said, handing Danelle a can of mace.

"We'll go to his apartment with you after work, to make sure it's in a nice and safe area, and not where you can get taken advantage of," Aubry said.

"Okay, you two can come check out the apartment and then help me get my things from the old place," she said before they all focused on their backlogged work that accumulated during the chaos and conversation.

Chapter Eighteen

Danelle, Kim and Aubry took off an hour early, allowing them to check out the apartment. Aubry and Kim were skeptical, having their friend's best interest at heart. The address he sent was located in Enola, Pennsylvania, alongside the Susquehanna River. When she pulled up to the building with the address, he gave her, she couldn't believe it. "He's full of it, Danelle. He doesn't live here or have an apartment here," Aubry said, looking up at the twenty-five-story building boasting lavish condos, not apartments as he played it down.

"There's only one way to find out. If he doesn't have a place here, then I'll text him back for the right address," Danelle said as they were walking toward the entrance.

The doorman nodded his head at the ladies while opening the door. "Welcome to M & W Condos, ladies. Can I direct you anywhere?"

"Yes, please. Where is apartment 2520?"

"There isn't any apartment numbered 2520," he responded.

"I told you this is the wrong place," Aubry said.

"However, ma'am 2520 is a sky loft. Take the first elevator to your left, but you must have a card along with the key, so stop at the desk," the doorman stated.

The ladies all made their way to the front desk a slim red-haired female stood behind, looking youthful in her early thirties, very classy, favoring Julia Roberts. "How may I help you ladies?" she asked.

"I'm going up to room 2520, but the doorman said I need a card to scan in order to get to that floor," Danelle said.

"You do, because it's a private floor. Give me one second," she said before picking up the phone and making a call.

"Excuse me sir, there are three young ladies here requesting a card to access the twenty-fifth floor. Okay, I'm sorry. I'll take care of it." She hung the phone up and activated a card before asking, "Which one of you is Ms. Dupri?" All of the ladies were shocked that she knew her name.

"I'm Danelle Dupri. How did you know my name?"

"Look around, Ms. Dupri. This building is high tech. The people who designed it are techies. So, my employees keep me and other staff informed. I hope you find the loft accommodating. If there is anything you need, we're here for you."

"I don't know about you and Kim, but I'm ready to see this loft," Aubry said.

"I'm still trying to figure out how Fuzzy Beard can even afford to live here, or not live here and live elsewhere," Kim said as Danelle turned the key and scanned the card.

"He could come from money or invested his money wisely. He does work hard and smarter than everyone at AmeriLink," Danelle said.

As they entered the elevator, an automated voice greeted her. "Welcome, Ms. Dupri. Will you and your guests be needing any beverages when you enter the loft?"

"I wish my house was like this," Kim said, looking around at the mirrored walls in the elevator, with digital touch everything.

"Three apple martinis, please."

"Request acknowledged."

The elevator doors parted on the twenty-fifth floor, revealing sumptuous marble floors throughout the ten thousand-square-foot loft. It had a fireplace and plush white leather furniture, surrounded by gold statues, end tables, and picturesque art on the walls that looked expensive, from Sotheby's Auction House in London.

"Ladies, your drinks are over here," a female voice came through the air. She stood in black attire, with a white shirt underneath, looking very professional. "I'm Shailynn, and I'll be your in-house chef and server. It has been a while since we've had guest here, so it is my pleasure to wait on you and your company, Ms. Dupri. Will you be needing dinner prepared?" she asked as each of them were still processing all of this, especially the portrait like view overlooking the Susquehanna River, staring back at Harrisburg's skyline on the other side of the river. Especially at night, it would be a breathtaking view.

"My daughter will be joining me for dinner. My friends came to make sure I'm okay."

"Would you like anything specific for dinner?"

"Italian food will be fine."

"Would you like a bottle of wine to compliment the meal?"

"Yes, please."

The chef nodded before vanishing over to the kitchen area. The ladies made their way over to the floor to ceiling window, taking in the view.

"Fuzzy Beard will have to explain all of this. It's nice, but who can afford to live here other than the bigwigs at work?" Kim said.

"I'm grateful for this gesture of him allowing me and Melanie to stay here, but my curiosity is piqued wanting to know why we don't have a place like this and how he invested his money to get it," Danelle said.

"If he didn't like you in a special way, you would be homeless right now. Instead, you're living like you hit the lottery," Aubry said.

"Five point five million is what this place is worth," the chef said, hearing Aubry's excitement as she approached. "What time would you like dinner to be served, Ms. Dupri?"

"Six will be fine," she said. The chef nodded before heading back to prepare dinner.

"Five point five million, Fuzzy Beard is rich. Why would he be working with us?" Aubry wondered as she followed Kim and Danelle to the large bedrooms.

"Company stocks he cashed out? He has been working there longer than all of us," Danelle said, also wanting to know more. As they were looking on at the loft, Danelle's phone chimed with an incoming message. She tapped the screen, seeing it was from Jay. It read: "I hope you find comfort in this place. More important, I hope your daughter likes it, too, especially since she has to move again.

Danelle: THANK YOU so much. I have questions on how you can afford this place, but that's another day and time. I appreciate your kindness. My daughter will too. C U @ work.

Jay: I composed something special for you, when you're not around Kim and Aubry. Read tonight please. C U @work.

Within minutes another text came in from Jay. As promised, she would read it tonight, when she was alone to think and process it all.

"Who was that?" Kim asked, seeing Danelle becoming quiet with a partial smile on her face.

"Jay asked if I liked this place and if it is okay for Melanie too."

"He's so cute, nerdy, and mysterious," Aubry said. "He knows this is more than enough, just being modest. We should help him find someone, since he's so nice to us."

"I think he has his eyes on Danelle," Kim said.

"He's nice and deserves happiness, with a good heart like his. I think he would turn down all the girls we picked for him," Danelle said.

"That's twice today you said he's so nice and will find someone. Are you secretly crushing on Fuzzy Beard?" Aubry asked.

"Really?" Danelle said, rolling her eyes before sipping her martini. "I have to go and get my daughter from school, plus you ladies need to help me get some things from my old place," Danelle said, ending the talk about her as they exited the loft.

Chapter Nineteen

8:47 p.m.

Danelle and Melanie settled into their new surroundings. Melanie was in her new big bedroom on the computer FaceTiming the boy from school, filling him in on the new temporary place. Danelle found herself in the living room, on the couch, listening to Sade's "Someone to Love" as she stared out at the city of Harrisburg's night skyline, having thoughts about her life, how she had ended up here in this very space, wondering what God's plan for her was.

"Here's your glass of red wine, Ms. Dupri. Will you be needing anything else this evening?"

"That'll be all for tonight. Thank you for everything, Shailynn."

"You're welcome. Will you be needing an early or late breakfast in the morning?"

"Early, with Melanie having to be at school by eight."

"Any special request?"

"She loves turkey bacon with scrambled eggs; me, I'm a pork and fried eggs girl," Danelle said, sipping her wine.

"It'll all be ready when you open your eyes," she said before retiring for the night in the chef's quarters. Danelle was now alone and accessed the message from Jay. She opened it, and the top read: "MORE THAN FRIENDS." She was intrigued by the caption, and she continued on to read the poem:

Danelle, I want to be more than friends, but first, I want to emotionally lure you in. Allow my words to be the hands that reach out to comfort you. Open your mind, so your heart can flow to the rhythm of my words, allowing me to be one with you. Together, we can paint this picture of a promising future how we please. You can get the passion you deserve as I cater to your needs. I need you to experience the other side of me. As more than friends, you can trust that I'll keep your secrets. I'll listen to you and your heart, so in return, you'll have something beautiful you can believe in. We can get lost in each other's presence. Danelle, seeing you each day is a gift in itself. It would be a loss if we didn't take advantage of this opportunity, or should I call it a blessing?

She took a gulp of her wine after readings this poignant poetry. It was so sweet, she thought, but she was still trying to figure out how to react to it. She never had looked at him that way. At the same time, she knew he had all of moral, mental, and emotional traits needed. So many thoughts were running through her mind. Now she understood why he asked that she read this alone. Aubry and Kim wouldn't allow her to fully focus on it, or her thoughts and emotions about then poem. She noticed at the bottom of the message there was an icon that read: "Click if YES For More Than Friends. NO to delete all." She took another gulp of her wine in between looking out at the skyline, then back to her phone with her thumb hovering over NO to delete all. At the same time, every conversation she had had with him entered her mind. How his words had gotten her through the hard times with leaving Trevor. How he protected her from Trevor. A part of her knew if she said NO, he would look at her different, maybe even feel embarrassed for his attempt. If she said YES, what would change? She placed the phone down, not ready to decide. Then she made her way over to the mini bar and took out a bottle of vanilla Cîroc vodka, pouring a double shot while laughing at the thoughts she was having of her and Jay being a thing. She took the double shot and downed it before refilling it. This one she carried back over to the couch. She picked her cell phone up, thumb over the icon. "This better be worth it, Jay," she said, tapping the screen for "YES more than friends." Her heart started beating now committing to this new thing, not judging him for looks, solely on what he brought and what a woman genuinely needs. Then screen went blank for a few seconds before Jay's face popped up.

"Hello, beautiful. I knew you would press yes, because AmeriLink's dating site rated us at a 99.5 percent connection in all areas. This is why I always appreciate each conversation we have and expressing my truth to you, hoping to guide you in the direction." He paused as if he was holding something back. Danelle was sitting there smiling at how nervous he seemed. "Okay, since you chose to be more than friends with me, I believe honesty is always best from the beginning. No lies, games, or deception. So, with that said. I want to tell and show you something."

The video cut off briefly only to start back up seconds later with Jay clean-shaven and good-looking, with his hair groomed and combed back, not greasy as he wore it at work. He looked like he could be a male model, favoring a mature Scott Disick and wearing an expensive navy-blue tailored suit, with glowing blue eyes, a radiant smile, and perfect white teeth, not the braces he normally wore as his disguise. The crazy thing was, as she was looking on at this refined, sexy man on her screen, it still hadn't registered that it was Jay like the letter J, but not in character. "How do I look, Danelle?" he asked.

"Damn, you look sexy," she blurted out as if he could hear her on this prerecorded video.

The video continued on, "My name is James Michaels. I'm the CEO and founder of AmeriLink. No one has seen me since I founded this company. As you may know by now, I'm one of the richest men in the world. So finding someone that likes you for you, when you have that much money, is hard to do. Besides, I went undercover at my company to be hands-on, along with hiding in plain sight. I found great interest in you hearing your daily conversations. And I would have fired you all if you weren't good at your jobs." She laughed at his words, still shocked by his reveal. "Danelle, I want to treat you and cater to you, as God intended a man to do for that one special woman. This means your baby girl will also be spoiled, sharing all I have to give, mentally, emotionally, physically, and financially. Oh, under one condition: I'm not ready to reveal my true identity to anyone else until I figure out a few more things. Oh, one other thing: Aubry is dating my associate, Mr. West. We own the building you're in along with many other investments. She doesn't know about me. He knows not to tell her. When the time comes, the world will see me. I know you're ready to take the next step in this life with me; otherwise, you wouldn't have pressed YES. With that said, be good to yourself and have a good night and even better dreams." The video came to an end, leaving her with so many thoughts and emotions, trying to process the reveal, at the same time excited that she did, with his sexy model look. She tried to replay the video, but he had encrypted it to delete after being played, so she wouldn't have a chance to reveal who he was in secret to her friends, or if someone else got a hold of her phone. Danelle downed the double, allowing all this newfound info to absorb into mind. Having to keep his secret would also add intrigue to what they had.

"This is going to be an exciting emotional ride," Danelle said, standing up and laughing at the visual of Jay like the letter J turning into sexy and sophisticated model James Michaels. This was definitely mind blowing, in a good way, making her look forward to all he had to bring. She was also thanking God for strategically aligning the two of them to cross paths as they did.

Chapter Twenty

7:01 a.m.

The chef made her rounds, awaking Danelle and Melanie to start their day with breakfast in bed. "If you need anything else, let me know," Shailynn said.

"Get me an excuse to not go to school today, so I can enjoy this nice place," Melanie responded.

The chef laughed, making her way over to Danelle's room and swiping her ID across the master suite's keypad, which allowed the computer to announce her presence, so they wouldn't be alarmed.

"Ms. Dupri, it's time to wake up for your breakfast as you requested," the automated female voice said. Danelle opened her eyes, thanking God again that she wasn't dreaming about being here or that video she'd seen last night with Jay's reveal. "Will you be taking your car to work, or should I have a driver ready?" At first, she wanted to have a driver take her to work, but then she would have to explain this to Aubry and Kim. Not a good start to keeping his secret. It was bad enough they were curious about how he was able to afford this place.

"You can have the driver take Melanie to school. I'll use my own car today."

"Should I prepare Melanie lunch for school?"

"I think she'll love that, Shailynn."

After the chef left, Danelle indulged in her breakfast as thoughts of Jay entered her mind, the sexy version of him, his word play, and promises of the better future they would share.

After breakfast, she made her way into work, smiling inside and out, feeling good about this new path she was taking. Aubry and Kim each noticed her glow, piquing their curiosity.

"Something is going on, Kim. Look at her face," Aubry said then added, "Tell me you didn't let Fuzzy Beard sneak over last night?"

"No, no, crazy. Your mind is always racing to the freaky things," Danelle responded as her head drifted toward Jay's direction, who had his back turned toward the women, working on his computer.

"Something happened, because her whole head just went on a swivel as she responded," Kim said, noticing Danelle's movements.

"I promise you, nothing happened other than me enjoying drinks alone, appreciating the nightlit skyline."

"Okay, no pressure on you, but I should go over and ask him how he can afford that place," Aubry said, knowing how much they made a year, which was low six figures.

"Come on, Aubry, let's go check him out," Kim said, edging the wild Aubry on, making their way over to him with chairs to sit close to him.

He leaned back in his chair, wondering what they were doing. "Uh oh, licky lick lips is back with her friend pretty Kim. You ladies should be working, not lounging like it's break time," he said, looking past them over at Danelle, who was standing there with her arms folded, shaking her head.

"Good morning, Jay," Kim said, trying to warm up to him.

"Okay, good morning pretty Kim and Aubry that likes to lick her lips in a seductive manner," he responded, making them laugh.

"First, we thank you for being so nice and a gentleman to our friend Danelle, allowing her to stay at your apartment that's really a loft," Aubry said.

"Oh, I see. You think I want something in return. No, no, I'm just being nice. If you don't think so, you should let her stay with you," he tossed out, shifting it back to them.

"That's not a problem, but there is plenty of room at your place you don't stay at anymore. Why is that? Do you have a bigger place? How can you even afford that place?" Aubry said, keeping the questions coming.

"I, I can't afford anything like that. It's too expensive. My grandfather left it for the family to share, but I'm the only one who has ever been there. That's too much for me. There are computer voices taking to you, and people present all the time. I like my privacy," he said, looking back and forth at Kim and Aubry, hoping they caught the hint about him liking his privacy. Jay really did have another place, that was small, that went along with his undercover role. He even drove a small electric car, not wanting to stand out.

"Ladies, he's answered your questions. Now come back over here so we can talk about Kim's new internet love interest and the two Tonys," Danelle said, trying to get them away from Jay. Jay sat pressing his glasses up on his nose looking at the ladies in between secretly appreciating Danelle. She flashed back to his sexy look in the video, which was a total transformation from this look with the braces, fake acne, fuzzy beard, and glasses. Keeping his secret added to the level of intrigue, making her gravitate toward him even more. The ladies got up, heading back over to their workstation.

"You're hiding something behind that smile, Danelle," Aubry stated. Danelle did not realize she was smiling, lost in her thoughts of last night's reveal, backed by his poetic words that further lured her in.

"So, what's going on with you and Mr. West?" Danelle asked, shifting the attention from her and Jay.

The thought of Anthony shifted Aubry's demeanor, making her feel so good, thinking of their first night together, his touch, the stimulation, the euphoria created by the emotional rush—a rushing feeling that took her heart and body by storm, allowing her to feel loved and appreciated. "We're going on a little trip this weekend, back by Monday he said," Aubry stated, lighting up in love.

"Private jet with two Tonys, how sexy and romantic is that?" Kim said.

"I know but let me say this: the black guy thing is true, so little Tony doesn't travel with me anymore. I have the real Tony that doesn't need me to guide it or hold it in place to please me," Aubry said, making the ladies and Fuzzy Beard laugh—mainly because it was his best friend she was talking about. He could only imagine how they would gossip when Danelle shared her stories of them together along with his reveal, when the time came. "So, what about your internet, boo Kim?" Aubry asked.

"All is well. I asked him if he wanted me to come to California to see him, but his job schedule is tying him up."

"Either he's catfishing you, or he has someone else," Aubry fired back.

"I've seen what he looks like when we use AmeriLink's close-up video time."

"Then he has someone else," Danelle said, knowing how slick men can be. "Next time you contact him, be straightforward and ask him if there's going to be anything more between you two. If not, move on."

"I agree, Kim, you can't get sex through the computer screen unless you're working your finger magic or have a toy that keeps you smiling while you're talking to him," Aubry said, being her usual self. Kim smiled at her words, knowing this was what she'd been doing.

"Don't worry, ladies, I have this all under control. Now let's focus on work before we get fired," Kim said. Jay gave a light laugh, reflecting back on what he said to Danelle about working.

As they tended to work, an email came through on Danelle's computer from Jay that read: "You look beautiful this morning. I'm glad you chose to be more than friends. I promise I won't let you or Melanie down. Oh, I didn't expect for your team of assassin girlfriends to attack me with questions. Would you like to do dinner at my place tonight?"

She smiled ear to ear, something Aubry noticed in between glancing at her screen. She didn't say anything, but she was curious who or what was making her smile like this.

Danelle: Dinner sounds fine, but I have a twelve-year-old daughter, remember?

Jay: If I come to your place, my place, our place, you know what I mean, I won't be able to be James Michaels. I would be Jay like the letter J.

Reading this became even more intriguing to her. Having the choice of two versions of her man was role play at its best.

Danelle: I'll have your star watch my daughter.

Jay: Texting you the address.

Each of them leaned back, taking in a glimpse of one another, loving the rush of their secret relationship.

Chapter Twenty-One

5:45 p.m.

Danelle was pulling up to the downtown address Jay gave her. For some reason her nerves kicked in, with this being her first official date, allowing another man into her life on a personal level. She double-checked her look in the rearview mirror before getting out. Her look for the evening was blue Dolce & Gabbana jeans with a white silk Prada shirt, lying on her perky 34C breast with slightly tweaked nipples, pressing against the shirt. Her fragrance was Gucci Pleasure. A light floral and sweet scent that was alluring. She made her way up to the apartment, knocking on the door. Jay answered the door with a smile, genuinely appreciating her presence and natural beauty. "Heaven has blessed me with you, an angel in the flesh," he said, taking her hand and welcoming her in.

"You look astonishing yourself, with the comfortable linen Armani loafers."

"I want you to see me as I really am, and not the guy at work," he responded, looking like a million dollars, well-groomed and refined. "Would you like anything to drink? I have sparkling water, wine, cognac, champagne, or soda," he added, leading the way to the dining room area.

"A shot of Patron Silver would be fine if you join me, so I won't be alone," she said, now seeing the table with white candles lit, flickering in sync with the music playing low. "Something smells good," she added while taking in all of the pristine decor.

"Almost as good as that sweet fragrance you're wearing. I'll have to remember that scent for a future gift," he stated, making a noticeable smile form on her face. "Tonight, I prepared us stuffed chicken parmesan. I took the portabella mushrooms, stuffing them into the breast, before seasoning them with homemade sauce and freshly grated parmesan. The sauce has a little red wine for bold flavor, which will make you smile as your taste buds are being caressed, melting over your tongue." His details on the preparation were making her hungry and turned on.

"Sounds good as its smells."

"Here's a shot for you, and one for me," he said, taking the time to lock eyes with hers, appreciating the sparkle in them. "Your eyes have this glow of life and happiness in them."

"I think we both have the sparkle, from what I can see in your eyes," she replied.

"We must be bringing out one another's true joy. Toast to a good dinner date, to getting to know one another on a personal outside of the workspace," he said, toasting his shot glass with hers. They downed the shots.

"That will take the nervous edge off," she said, handing him the empty glass.

"Really? I thought I was the only nervous one. Now I feel much better," he said as he started preparing their dinner plates. "Take a seat at the table. I'll bring over everything."

She did just that. Not long after, he came with the food, placing it on the small circular table for two.

"This is really good, Jay. Having skills like this in the kitchen, you don't need a chef."

"Thank you, Danelle. It's always nice when someone appreciates the work you put into something," he responded, cutting into his parmesan chicken. "So tell me something I don't know about you, that will allow me to get closer to you on a more intimate and personal level."

Her eyes raised up, looking on at him, ready to answer the question of interest that would allow them to form a mental and emotional bond. "I'm the only child, but I'm not spoiled as most would think. I fear not being a good mother, meaning not being able to provide a stable environment for my daughter. I fear being alone, without love, as much as I give it, when I'm with that one and only person. I love my job. I'm not just saying that because you own it. I do because it allows me to connect with people around the world. So, I feel like I'm helping someone at all times." She paused, taking a bite of the seasoned chicken and garlic pasta. Jay was cherishing and holding on to every word she spoke this far.

"Danelle, from this point on, you never have to worry about being alone or fear that Melanie will ever be in an unstable environment, as long as we know each other. As I presented to you in last night's video and text, I want to be more than friends. I want to be the reason behind your smile when you wake up each morning. I want to be the best thing that ever happened to you and Melanie. This isn't a mistake that we crossed paths. God's timing is unlike no other. However, it always seems to be the right time, when we understand it."

"I appreciate your comforting and reassuring words. Now it's your turn to tell me something about James Michaels."

"Like you, I'm the only child. My mother raised me alone. It wasn't always easy or pretty growing up, especially because she lost everything. We were homeless." A light laugh came out as he reflected back to his childhood memories. "We slept in a car for some time, until she got back on track. We never looked back, always forward, she always said, even until this day, with all that I have provided for us."

"Your mother, has she seen you in the last eight years?" she questioned, knowing he'd been hiding in plain sight.

"Of course, she wouldn't let me go that long without seeing her. Now you along with her and Anthony are the only ones who know my secret identity."

"When was your last relationship, since you live this secret life?"

"Right before I decided to live in disguise. Being a young billionaire, every female was throwing themselves at me. I thought I found love once, until I discovered otherwise, thanks to my technology, to see her true intent, along with always spending my money, like it was growing on trees."

It'd been a few months for her and eight long years for him. She hadn't even thought of sex since Trevor, because she was focused on bouncing back emotionally and mentally. "You know I'm not that type of female. I seek comfort in love, not money. I'm a woman that appreciates the institution of a relationship, honoring its meaning," she said.

Jay embraced her words as he sipped his wine, before sitting the glass down, extending his hand across the table, and sliding it on top of hers. For the first time in eight years, his hand was in contact with a female's flesh. Danelle's heart was warming at his touch, stimulating their thoughts and emotions, giving them this euphoric rush of butterflies, making this dinner unique, as they're coming alive.

"Danelle, I've waited eight years to meet you. I'm not going to let you, or all you have to offer, slip away."

The feeling she was having looking back at him was making her heart flutter. She stood from the table and walked over to him, placing her soft hand on his neck and caressing him with her French manicured nails. She leaned in, placing a kiss on his lips. His eyes briefly opened to look into her eyes before closing his to enjoy this passionate kiss. They parted from the kiss, now looking on at one another, thankful for this moment. "You saved me in so many ways, Jay. Thank you for coming into my life."

"The heart never lies, so I always speak the truth," he said, knowing his encouraging words had gotten them to this point. The conversation and kisses traveled to the living room, where they watched a movie and snuggled next to each other until they got lost in one another's kisses and heavy caressing. Each of them was turned on, since it'd been awhile. Jay kissed her neck while pressing gently up against her breasts, all her spots, making her horny and hot.

"That's nice, mmmmh," she let out, almost tickled by his touch and kisses to her neck. Hearing her light moan made his heart pound as his stiffness pressed hard up against his pants, close to her body. Her hands were rubbing up and down his leg, finding his long pulsating manhood trapped in his pants. She was impressed by his length, wanting to have fun with it now but remaining a lady, not wanting to give the goodies up on the first night. His hand was now sliding down to her belly, which was trembling at his touch, assisted by his lips on her neck. Now his hand was between her legs, pressing and rubbing up against her love spot, making her moan.

"Mmmmmmh, Jay, mmmmmmh." His heart was thumping even more, loving her touch as much as she was loving his. Her body was ready and wanting him to undress her. Even if she wanted to be a lady and not have sex on the first night, she wouldn't resist if it kept feeling this good. His fingers pressed up against her pants, stimulating her even more, making this foreplay intense. "Jay, Jay, that feels so good, mmmmh, mmmmh," she moaned, not having touched herself masturbating in the last four months. That area had been shut off, until now.

His lips came off her neck and close to her ear as he whispered, "I will always be good to you, your heart and body." His words melted her just as much as his fingers pressing against her pants, creating a rushing sensation that wanted to be released from her body. This feeling was making her want to come out of her clothes so he could take his time with her bare flesh.

At the same time, in her mind, knowing no matter how good it was feeling, she had to bring control over herself and this situation, to respect herself and the future of their relationship. "Jay, Jay. Mmm-mmmh. Okay, okay, that's enough for now. As much as I want more of your touch, I want it to also be special and not on our first night," she said, breathing a little heavier than normal, still feeling that sensation that wanted to be released with intense pleasure. She laughed, looking on at him, knowing he, too, wanted more, but he was patient.

"I look forward to our next date and time together. Besides, we have a future of foreplay and fun nights awaiting us," he said, placing a kiss on her soft lips. "It would be nice if you stayed the night, allowing me to wake up to your beautiful smile and face," he added.

"In time we'll have all that we please and more. I did enjoy every second of this first date. But right now, it's late. I have to get back to the loft before Melanie starts to worry. Keep in mind, I couldn't tell her where I was going."

"A night of juicy details for your girlfriends?" he tossed out there.

"I wish, but this will stay between us until you're ready," she said as he walked her to the door. "Good night, sexy man."

"Good night, beautiful. Drive safe," he said, kissing her once more before she walked away. He closed the door, excited that he finally found the woman he would be honored to introduce to his mother. A woman that didn't care about his money, only the emotions he could bring into their relationship.

Danelle drove home with a smile from ear to ear, flashing back to his touch, the way it made her feel, the light moans and giggles as the sensation stirred in her body. Her heart, mind, and woman's intuition were also telling her that she made the right decision in saying, "Yes, more than friends," to him. Now she would have to contain this good feeling and Jay's secret, which added to this sub-rosa life she was living.

Chapter Twenty-Two

Friday came fast, something each of the ladies was looking forward to. Kim and her internet interest were planning to finally meet up in the Midwest, Chicago, at UNO deep dish pizza. They had both heard good things about the place, so they figured they would try it together. Danelle and Jay secretly made plans for the weekend to see each other in and out of character, depending on where they would meet. Aubry and Anthony West took his private jet to Paris, where they took time to see the lit-up Eiffel Tower.

"This is a beautiful structure that gives off a romantic vibe," Aubry said, staring up at the tower, holding his hand. Then she added, "Mr. Alexandre Gustave, a French engineer, had this vision that came together standing nine hundred and eighty-four feet tall, overlooking the beautiful skyline and the Seine River," impressing him with her knowledge.

"Someone was paying attention in school, or you did your research. Either way, I appreciate your intellect," Tony said.

She raised up on her toes, leaning in for a passionate kiss, loving his lips on hers. "Paris is an intimate and romantic place, but it is you that makes it special for me Tony," Aubry said in the moment, her eyes locked on his.

"Let's go to the top, baby, so we can say we had the full experience of the Eiffel Tower, the way it was intended," he said, taking her hand and leading the way. As they made their way to the top, they witnessed couples proposing, osculating, and embracing one another with love and affection. Tony, seeing this, held Aubry close, at the same time thinking about all he wanted with her and their future. "This is definitely the place you come to when your heart is in the right place, to embrace all of the intimate inspiration," Tony said, stirring an emotional cord in Aubry's heart, making her smile inside and out.

"You know I'm all yours, emotionally, physically, and mentally, plus Tyler thinks the world of you," Aubry stated, expressing herself while looking into his eyes with love. The moment of affection pulled each of them into a passionate kiss that seemed more special than any other they'd shared thus far. Her heart was fluttering with love and butterflies, melting into his warm embrace. Tony knew this woman was where his heart was and where he wanted to be in life. She deserved a ring, but doing it here would be cliche, so he was going to wait for the right time. Aubry started taking pictures at the top of the Eiffel Tower with her and Tony, followed by selfies. She sent pics to her best friends, wanting them to how beautiful it was, along with how romantic her man was. After spending time at the tower, they made their way over to a five-star restaurant owned by chef Emeril Lagasse. The setting was romantic with a red-lit dining area, with Italian music being played in the background, accompanied by the aroma of fine Italian cuisine filtering through the air. Once they were seated, drinks and conversation flowed.

"Anthony, have you ever had anyone else you felt this good about, like I do you?" Aubry questioned. "Because the way I feel when I'm around you is so different than any man I've ever been in a relationship with. You make me come alive inside and out," she said, feeling committed to him one hundred percent. She took a sip of her Chateau du Busca Hors d'age. Tony always knew when she was serious, as she would say his full name instead of Tony. "Aubry, you're my one. The one who brings out a unique version of myself and body. Each second we share is more precious than those that have passed. Each second becoming its own cherished moment and memory that I'll hold onto forever, to remind me of why I want more of you," he responded, looking into her eyes, feeling this deep intimate connection that was making their hearts beat in sync for one another's love and affection.

Aubry, having a moment, had to wipe a tear from the corner of her eye, feeling his words that reached deep, caressing her heart. "Don't think I'm crazy and leave me here eating alone. It's you I want now and forever. It doesn't take long for the heart to guide you in the right direction, especially when these good, never before feelings take over whenever you're near or when I think of you," Aubry expressed with an open heart, no holding back.

"I love you, Aubry," he said for the first time, wanting her to know he mirrored the way she was feeling.

"You do? I mean, I love you, too, and I was trying to say it without sounding crazy or obsessed," she said, laughing a little.

"From the moment in the elevator, when I first crossed paths with you, I knew I wanted to be with you and know more about how to cater to you and your heart," he said, standing up and making his way around to her side of the table, taking her hand and pulling her close for a hug, before looking into her eyes. "Aubry, you want this life with me now and forever?"

"I only want you in my life, Anthony. My heart and goodies are for you only," she responded, making him laugh lightly.

He turned around, looking at the people in the restaurant enjoying their food and vacation. "Excuse me, everyone, for one second please. I want the world to know I really love this woman right here," he said, making Aubry smile. She was shocked in a good way, as her heart and mind were racing, feeling appreciated by this man. He turned to face her. "Aubry Marie Marching, I want you to be my morning smile and my nighttime comfort before I close my eyes to sleep. I want you to share all of me with you, so together we can make this love more than a dream. So, will you marry me?" Aubry's heart and mind were wrapped in this romantic life changing moment as tears of joy and love flowed. Anthony got down one knee and presented a flawless 4.86 carat cushioned diamond, with radiant cut diamonds on each side along with pavé diamonds set in platinum. A ring that cost close to one million dollars, but for him, it wasn't about the price. He appreciated the beauty of the diamond, which was a reflection of his love and her beauty inside and out. Onlookers were snapping pictures, adding sparkle to the radiant diamond.

"Yes, yes, I will marry you any day or time. I love you, Anthony," Aubry said as he's slid the ring on her finger. Then he stood sealing the proposal with a passionate kiss as the people started clapping, watching this love story unfold. "Let's take a seat, my love," he said, kissing her once more before they sat down and continued with dinner. Within the hour they were back at the sumptuous suite. Aubry sat on the edge of the bed, excited with her phone. "I have to send a pic of this beautiful ring to my friends and let them know how much we love each other," she said, snapping away and sending the pictures that had the caption: "OMG I'm In LOVE!!! #Getting Married." It didn't take long before the best friends responded with just as much excitement as if they got proposed to.

Kim: Woooow! That thing is so BIG, it almost came through the screen. #Lucky you.

Danelle: Who would have thought, the wildest of the three would be getting hitched first? It looks amazing! Congratulations!

Aubry: I love you ladies. Now it's time to show my future hubby how much I luv him, byeee!!

Aubry sat her phone down and crawled over to Tony, taking the remote out of his hand, unbuttoning his shirt that exposed his bare, cut-up body with a tight six-pack. Her hands caressed his chest in between, placing kisses on his chest, then his stomach. At the same time her fingers opened his pants, sliding her hand into his silk boxer shorts, making his manhood come alive. Her lips trailed over his stomach, making him squirm from her intimate touch. She removed him from his pants, placing a kiss on the top. "I love you too," she said, talking to his manhood, making Tony laugh at how crazy she was. She removed his pants and boxers, tossing them to the side of the bed. She removed her clothing; the only thing she was wearing was the sparkling diamond engagement ring. She climbed on top of him, taking hold of his full erect thickness and raising up and placing the tip on her wet love place, ready to receive him. As she lowered down slowly, a light moan of passion escaped.

"Aaaah, Tony, I'm going to make love to you, baby," she said, being on top, taking control, and moving her hips slowly, gyrating up and down, looking into his eyes, adding to the intimate lovemaking. His hands were now reaching out, holding on to her hips, awaiting her up-and-down movement. "Aaaaah, Tony, baby. Aaaaah, aaaaah, I love this. Aaaaah," she said, going up and down, allowing all of his thick and long love stick to fill her up. At the same time, this new position of engagement was adding to this lovemaking. "Aaaaah, baby. Mmmmmmh, mmmmmmh, I want this to be special for you, Tony, baby. Mmmmmmh, you like that? Aaaaah, aaaaaaah." Aubry's heart, mind, and body were into this lovemaking session, allowing her body to react with intense surging orgasms that built up with each deep stroke of her pressing down on his love stick, filling up her body. "Aaaaah, aaaaah, right there, baby. You like this?

Aaaaah, aaaaah, mmmmmh, mmmmh. Ooooh baby, oooooh, I love you, Tony. Oooooh, oooooh, aaaaah, aaaaah." Her movement were picking up, and she rode him harder and faster as intense waves of pleasure rushed through her body. At the same time, she could feel him pulsating, also ready to erupt. This was turning her on even more. Now feeling the uncontrollable powerful surge racing through her body, she leaned forward with her lips against his ears, moaning, turning him on even more, making him thrust deeper and harder into her body. "Tony, baby, mmmmmmh, mmmmmmh. Mmmmmmh, ooooh, baby. Oooooh, baby," she let out as the orgasmic sensation soared through her body, escaping with intense pleasure, to the point that her moans turned into love bites on his neck and shoulder. He was turned on by her love bites as he erupted, feeling the love and passion.

Her love bites shifted to his chest, stimulating him even more, making his manhood stay at attention. At the same time, she continued gyrating her hips, loving this feeling of making love to him, to show her appreciation for their relationship and the diamond ring he gave her. "I love you, Tony. I will be a good wife and a freak to you in every way you desire," she said with a smile, still moving her hips in between placing love bites on his chest.

"I look forward to being your husband and your everything when you need me the most, emotionally, mentally, or physically, when your body is yearning for mine," he said, pulling her close for kisses before turning her over, allowing him to now take control over this lovemaking session. "You ready for round two?" he asked guiding her to turn over on her belly, his kisses trailing down her back over her bottom, where he placed a love bite, getting a light giggle out of her. His kisses trailed back up before he entered from behind, creating a euphoric high that stimulated her heart and mind, making her love and appreciate him even more. Their intimate session lasted through the night, enhancing their love for one another.

Chapter Twenty-Three

Monday came, and the ladies couldn't wait to see one another, to share their juicy details of their weekend. Danelle would be the only one concealing how her weekend really went, even with the level of excitement and good she was feeling inside. Jay stayed in character, taking Danelle and Melanie to Hershey Park. Melanie thought he was weird at first, but cute and funny. She had no clue that her mother's new friend was one of the world's richest men. Danelle entered the office with Jay trailing behind her, but not looking like a couple.

"Good morning, ladies," Jay said before making his way over to his workstation. Aubry zoomed in on him and Danelle. His demeanor and glow were different, just as hers was. A part of Aubry thought they must be a thing, but he was not her type, so that thought slipped away.

"What's your happy glow about, Danelle?" Aubry asked.

"I was just checking out you and that beautiful ring. Let me see," Danelle said as Aubry extended her hand, giving her a close up. "I love it; it's shiny and beautiful."

"That's what I said, in between the love making session to show my appreciation."

"I'm surprised you are not still humping on him, with a big ass ring like that," Kim said, making them laugh, including Jay.

"He is the one for me, as I am for him. We found the balance in each other."

"Kim and I can't wait to go dress shopping with you, whenever you set the date."

"I want a spring or summer wedding, so we can have pretty flowers and an outdoor setting," she said, warmed by the thoughts of her big day. "Not to get off of the happy wedding trail, but Kim, how was your weekend with Mr. Internet?"

"It was good. We spent time in Chicago, sharing our first deep pie. You ladies need to take a trip there. The food is worth it."

"Skip the deep dish, cut to the goods. Does he look good in person? Is he a good kisser? Did you give him the goodies?" Aubry said, not wasting any time.

Kim turned blush red, thinking about how her weekend ended with this man.

"What's his real name?" Danelle asked, knowing he only went by a screen name.

"Ricardo Rodriguez," Kim responded.

"The Spanish language is so sexy. I know it turned you on," Aubry said.

Kim lit up thinking about it. "I can say when we kissed, I felt lifted from the ground. That's how explosive the kiss was. We ate pizza, and then he ate a little more," she said, getting both of their attention.

"You bad, bad girl, Kim," Danelle said.

"I never had anything like that happen to me before, the way his lips, tongue, and fingers seemed to caress all of my body. It was so good I almost fell out of the bed, squirming, trying to embrace it all," she said, making them laugh. "We didn't go any further, not that I needed to after he put his oral gifts to use."

"Don't tell me you stopped him?" Aubry said.

"No, no, yes. I was so overwhelmed with powerful orgasms; I couldn't take anymore. I just wanted him to lie there and hold me." Hearing her say this made

Danelle and Aubry shake their heads, smiling at how he had their friend twisted.

“I know you can’t wait to see him again, from the sounds of it,” Danelle said.

“He’s coming here to visit me this Friday, staying for the weekend.”

“I’m so glad he is what you expected and more,” Danelle said.

“Yes, he is,” she responded, closing her eyes briefly, flashing back to the erotic moment she shared with him. Ricardo, her internet love interest, also works for Newtech.com a California based company.

Jay glanced over at Danelle and her friends gossiping. Right then she knew it was time to get back to work, as Jay prided himself on being number one in this business by staying competitive. “We can pick this up over our lunch break. We have to get to work now.”

“Okay, boss lady,” Aubry said, being sarcastic. As soon as the ladies typed in their access codes to get into the computer, an alert came over everyone’s screen on the floor at the same time. The supervisor came out fast from the back.

"Listen up, everyone. There is an attempt being made to hack into our system. Our counter hack is reversing and tracing the origin of the idiot who attempted this! No one can leave until this process is figured out!"

"I can't stay here all day," Aubry said, discouraged by the thought.

"It shouldn't take all day," Kim said.

"We're locked out of our computers, no work, so we'll be backlogged when they do come back up," Danelle said. At the same time, Jay looked up over his shoulder. His eyes were searching the women, until Aubry noticed him.

"What are you doing over there, Fuzzy Beard?" Aubry asked.

"Nothing, I, I just can't get any work done with this hack thing. I wonder why someone would do this?" he responded.

"This company is the powerhouse in this business, with cutting-edge technology, staying ahead of the rest, so the competition will do anything to get a glimpse at what's behind these walls," Aubry responded.

"It's crazy if they think AmeriLink isn't prepared for things like this. They think ten moves ahead, like in chess," Jay said.

"I hope that's true, Jay like the letter J, because I don't want to be without a job," Aubry said. Even if she was with a wealthy man, she didn't mind working.

"Wow, that's a nice ring. Is it heavy on your hand?" Jay asked.

"Thank you. No, it isn't heavy, it is very nice. I'm in love, Jay, and maybe one day you will be too," Aubry responded.

Danelle heard her words, making her smile inside and out. "I'll find her and never let her go, just watch," he said as Aubry headed back to her station. He locked eyes with Danelle briefly, enjoying the excitement of their secret. They all sat waiting for the computers to come back on. They couldn't even use their cell phones. That was another built-in feature for whenever the system detected a hack; it shut down all cell phone use. Aubry noticed that one person was using a cell phone. How? she wondered as she looked on at Jay.

"How is Jay the only one with cell phone service during this secured locked down?" Aubry asked.

"Let's go find out," Kim said. They made their way over to him.

"Jay like the letter J, how are you able to use your phone when no one else can?" Aubry asked.

Hearing the question stunned him, knowing in this secured lockdown, no one else's phones were working. He had created this security, which allowed him to encrypt his phone for emergencies like now. He couldn't tell them this. He was on the phone with his partner Anthony West, who had been at the airport ready to fly out on business. Now he was heading to AmeriLink. "This thing doesn't work. I was just messing around with it. I see I fooled you, huh?"

"You're lying, Jay. I saw you talking," Aubry said, standing firm.

"Uh oh, licky lips is steaming. I'm not a liar; no I'm not. It's my phone; it doesn't work."

"You could be the reason behind the hack," Kim said, eyeing him down. He pressed his glasses up on his nose, looking on at her.

"I, I seriously doubt that, pretty Kim. I gain nothing from trying to cheat anyone, especially this place.

AmeriLink has been good to me," he said, looking past the women to see Danelle slightly upset with her friends' antics.

"Aubry, Kim, JAY is our friend. He would never do a thing like that. Besides, the company will figure it out." As those words came out of her mouth, the boss came back out, looking in their direction.

"Ms. Miles, can you come with me, please?" the boss said, speaking to Kim, who was looking shocked, questioning what was wrong.

"Is there something wrong, sir?" she asked in fear of losing the job she loved.

"We're trying to figure that out," he said, heading to the back. At the same time, Mr. West exited the elevator accompanied by two AmeriLink security guards. Aubry knew something was wrong when he looked over at her. She started feeling as if he thought she had something to do with this hack.

"Is everything okay, baby?" she asked.

"I hope so, my love," he said, briefly coming over to place a kiss on her lips. "I really hope so."

He didn't want to think that his future wife and best friend were trying to hack his company for information that would be worth hundreds of millions, even billions depending on the technology leaked. He headed to the back, getting a quick head nod from Jay. Once in the back, the questions came.

"Ms. Miles, it's your security code that has been used from another location that has led to this attempted hack to access AmeriLink files and data."

"Whatever you're trying to say, I love my job, and I wouldn't do anything to jeopardize it," she said nervously, wondering how someone got her code.

"Ms. Miles, I'm Mr. West, an associate here. My tech guys tell me that though it is your code, someone is riding on it to access information in our system. We have narrowed it down, tracing the link to California, where most of our competition is. We'll have the exact person responsible for this soon. Are you in any way involved in this?"

"Hell no! I told you, I love my job," she responded, wiping her tears.

"Who has access to your codes and why?" Mr. West questioned.

"No one. I wouldn't give that out."

"Have you ever used our system for personal use that may have allowed someone to come in?" Mr. West asked.

She didn't want to admit that she had used her personal computer to go online to check the dating sites as well as shop while at work. Either one would be grounds to fire her. As she was preparing to respond with a lie, it came to her. Ducking Ricardo Rodriguez! He worked at the competition. What if it was him? That meant all the nice things he said to her were lies just to get access to AmeriLink. Her mind was racing as her heart was aching thinking this could be true. "Yes. I used it for shopping and dating sites."

"Who stood out to you on those dating apps?" he asked, making her think of the person who paid her the most attention, showing intimate interest: Ricardo Rodriguez. That motherfucker, she thought, feeling this sharp pain in her heart.

"Ricardo Rodriguez. He works at Newtech.com in California."

Hearing this made red flags pop up, confirming what they had figured out already. Now Mr. West was thinking she was either in on it or too naive and lacking the competence to protect AmeriLink, since they trusted her with the codes and access to the system. "Ms. Miles, these men here will be escorting you out. Your personal things at your station will be forwarded to your address," Mr. West said, crushing her even more.

"No, no, I didn't do anything wrong. Please don't do this to me," she said, breaking down crying as she was escorted through the office area. Aubry and Danelle saw this and became worried.

"Anthony, what's going on? Why are these men walking my best friend out?" Aubry asked, rushing over to her fiancé, stopping him in his tracks.

At the same time, Kim responded to her, "They think I had something to do with the hack. That son of a bitch Ricardo scammed me, using me to get in." She was crying hard. Aubry and Danelle embraced her.

"She can't leave. You can't fire her, Mr. West. She didn't do anything wrong," Danelle said.

"There's been a breach in security that she willingly or unwillingly became a part of. My actions at this point are protocol," he responded.

Right then Danelle made eye contact with Jay, wanting him to step in, to say something, to save her best friend. Kim would never break the law or do anything to lose her job. Danelle, feeling the pain of her friend being escorted out, couldn't contain her emotions. "Jay! Please don't let them do this to my friend!" she blurted out. Her words stunned everyone around, wondering who she was talking to. Mr. West knew, which is why he froze in the moment. Aubry was still unaware but wondering why her friend was calling out to Jay. Jay pressed his glasses up on his nose, turning the other way, as if tending to something else, not wanting to break cover. "She leaves, we leave, too, Aubry," Danelle said.

Jay heard her words, which stung his heart, because he really cared for Danelle, but she had to understand this business was his life and legacy. Jay, torn in the moment, quickly sent a text message to Mr. West, his associate.

Jay: Get rid of the security guards. Instruct every one else to take the rest of the day off.

Instantaneously Tony received the message that was sent discreetly. He read the text, feeling some weight being lifted off of him, especially with his future wife being involved.

"Gentlemen. I can take it from here. Everyone here can have the rest of the day off, including you, Ms. Miles," he said with a brief smile, looking at his fiancé, knowing he made her happy with his decision, thanks to his associate Jay's fast thinking. Danelle noticed Jay sliding his phone back into his pocket. She knew right then he sent the message to him. He turned back around, nodding his head at her, seeing her smile as a way of thanking him.

Chapter Twenty-Four

6:01 p.m. Eastern Time

The FBI detained Ricardo Rodriguez and his employers for questioning. Kim was also questioned, before they let her go, thanks to Jay, Danelle, and Aubry, who were at her side. Kim was feeling the betrayal, being deceived by Ricardo. His true intent was to get info for his company, even if this meant getting close and intimate with her. Kim ended up going home to drink and cry her pain away. Danelle was at the high-rise with Melanie awaiting Jay's arrival, since he had to secure some other things with the company and his associate Mr. West. Aubry was at her place waiting to hear from her fiancé since he was busy with the investigation of the hack at the company. She sent out a message to Kim, who she was feeling for, knowing she gave her all to that relationship that abruptly ended with deception.

Aubry: Don't give up on love. It's Ricardo's loss. You're a smart, sexy beast.

She put smiley faces and heart emojis with hopes of cheering up her friend.

Kim: U R crazy, but I'm off of the luv train for now. It almost cost me my job.

Aubry: We would have tracked his ass down, if the FBI didn't.

Kim found laughter in her words, knowing how true they were.

Kim: About to have another shot of Hennessey to calm myself.

Aubry: Treat yourself to the bottle. You had a rough day, girl.

Kim: LOL SMH, I'm so glad you reached out. I needed this pick-me-up.

Aubry: I love you, but Tony just came through the door, byeeee.

"Aubry, babe, I'm sorry how things went today at the office. That's the business side of me," he said, coming over to her with open arms, allowing her to fall into his embrace with a kiss.

"I understand. I know Kim doesn't have a criminal bone in her body, so I had to stand by my girl," she said, placing another kiss on his lips before adding, "Are you hungry, babe?"

"I'm starving. What are we having?" he asked.

"You can have me, if you're really starving," she said playfully, bringing a smile to his face.

"I made spaghetti and meatballs, the old fashion way from scratch."

"After dinner we can take a shower together, watch a movie, and enjoy each other's space. I can't get enough of your Italian loving," he said, making her feel even more appreciated by his love.

"Mmh, is this foreplay, the way you're looking and taking to me. If so, I'm enjoying it," she said, looking up at him with lust and love in her eyes, smiling before turning heading to the kitchen, allowing him to enjoy the sight of her perfect shaped bottom walking away.

A few seconds passed before he followed. "I want you to think about leaving AmeriLink, so we can focus more on us and our future," he stated.

"Why? I like being able to gossip with my friends about how much I love my future husband, as well as hearing their stories," she responded.

He came up behind her and placed his hand on her hips as he leaned in and placed a kiss on her neck. "You still can do all of that, but not as an employee. I'm going to take care of you in every way for the rest of your life. You and Tyler are my world, and I want it to always be this way, without any problem, as there was today, to compromise my business and/or relationship. It put me in a bad place today, having to protect my business while being serious with the one I love," he stated, making her understand his position and reason for asking this of her.

"You know my girls are going to be so mad at me for this, but for our love, I'm willing to consider it. You better never leave either, or I want my job back," she said, making light of the situation.

"I'm not going anywhere, so you're stuck with me showing you a whole new world of life and ways to love," he said, caressing her heart with his words. "Now let's eat. I'm hungry."

"Taste this, babe," Aubry said, dipping her finger into the sauce and bringing it to his lips, his mouth opening, taking her finger in seductively, more foreplay for tonight's ending.

"Mmh hmm, this is good, babe."

Aubry was stimulated by his tongue on her finger, but she contained herself so they could get through dinner. "Now go have a seat. I'll bring your plate out. What do you want to drink?" she asked.

"Surprise me, babe," he said, tapping her bottom before leaving the kitchen. She glanced over her shoulder, thinking, "I really love this man."

While Aubry and Tony enjoyed dinner, across town, Danelle was making her way out to meet Jay at the elevator opening in the loft. Even the in house chef was standing there with his requested beverage. Melanie was in her room getting ready for dinner, in between finishing up a call with her friend from school. The doors parted, and both Danelle and Shailynn were shocked. The chef had always seen

Jay as Fuzzy Beard. At the same time Danelle didn't expect him to show up as himself, in this two-piece Armani soft silk suit, tailored to perfection, showing the outline of his fit frame, and clean-shaven, enhancing his million-dollar bright white smile. His glowing eyes now filled with love and affection for Danelle, a look that she noticed as her eyes locked with his. His watch matched the tone of his suit, an Asprey Entheus R2 GMT with the blue face set with rose gold and a blue alligator band. A limited edition, only a few people in the world had one.

"I didn't expect this version of you today," Danelle said, still appreciating him no matter how he showed up.

"I don't want to hide anymore, especially after finding a woman that makes me feel so good inside and out." His words found her heart. She placed a kiss on his lips, showing her appreciation for his words and emotions. "After what took place today, it brought things into perspective for me. I never want to see you hurt as you were with your ex or as you were seeing what took place with your friend."

"I do thank you for helping her," Danelle said, kissing him again. At the same time Melanie came in, never having seen this good-looking man who was kissing her mom.

"Mom! Not cool. Jay wouldn't approve of this!" Melanie said, unaware that she was kissing Jay since she had never seen him out of character. Jay started laughing, realizing Melanie didn't recognize him.

"Mel, this is Jay, the real James Michaels. He's no longer in character."

Melanie's eyes widened hearing his real name, as she knew who he really was and that he hadn't been seen in years. She also knew he was one of the richest men in the world and was considered a genius in many circles.

"OMG, stop playing. So this is the hotter version of yourself? I really like the other version, but this is so funny and too much right now," Melanie said, laughing and even more excited for her mother.

Jay came over to Melanie. "I'm still the same person you like. I'll be that and more for you and your mother," he said, opening his arms and embracing Melanie like a fatherly figure. "I'm here to love and protect you and your mother forever," he added, making happy tears come to Danelle's face, feeling this weight of keeping his secret lifted from her.

Now she could share her true happiness with the world, but first, her girlfriends, who were going to go crazy when they found out Fuzzy Beard was *the* James Michaels. Danelle came over and rubbed his back lovingly. "You two ready to eat?" she asked.

"Yes, I am. Shailynn, can you bring me my drink please?" he asked. She obliged with his double shot of Henry XIII cognac, smooth aged. They all took a seat at the table, awaiting dinner.

"So, are you coming to work as Jay or James Michaels tomorrow?"

"No more Jay. I know you're going to miss Fuzzy Beard, as you ladies used to call me," he said, mocking them. She laughed knowing how true his words were.

"Are you going public, since the world hasn't seen you in a while?"

"In time. I have one more thing that needs to be taken care of. The world will know that I'm alive and well, thanks to the one woman I care about deeply, who made this possible."

"Thanks, Mom. You know a lot of kids at my school think he's dead and the government is running your business."

"Mel, you can't tell your friends about him until he's ready for the world to know. So, no tweets or Instagram postings, okay?"

"I got this, Mom. No one can keep a secret better than me."

"Oh really? What else are you keeping from me?" Danelle asked, concerned.

"Nothing, just know your secret is safe with me."

The dinner continued, allowing them to bond. Melanie slid off after dessert, allowing the two love birds time to themselves. They found their way to the couch, listening to Sade's "No Ordinary Love," a timeless love song that suited their situation, how it all came together, thanks to God's timing. Danelle was snuggled up against him, resting her head on his shoulder. Her hand caressed his chest affectionately. He kissed the top of her head, also feeling the moment. As they sat on the couch they could see through the floor-to-ceiling windows, out at the night-lit skyline of Harrisburg. After a few songs, they stood, making their way over to the window, holding hands.

"Danelle, baby, you see all of this, the view, the world out there?"

"Yes, it's beautiful. I enjoy this view every night."

"This view has no comparison of the view I have when I'm looking on at you or staring intimately into your eyes, cherishing your beauty, brains, and body that I'll forever appreciate. All of this out here—" he pointed outside "—it means nothing if it can't be shared with someone special, someone like you, who gets and understands me, way before you knew about my money or my true identity. I'm going to give you more than you've ever imagined in love and life," he said, downing his drink and placing the empty glass on the table by the flowers. His words pulled them in for an intimate kiss, followed by their roaming hands, stimulating their bodies. Suddenly, he parted from the kiss, taking control, turning her around and facing her out the window at the night sky.

His lips found her neck, placing erotic love bites that were turning her on. Her hands pressed against the glass as his free hand slid around unbuttoning her pants, before his masculine fingertips made their way over her perfect landing strip, caressing her pearl, making a light moan escape as her heart raced with excitement. "Mmmmh," she let out, feeling his fingers parting her and thrusting into her body. Her head leaned back with her hands still pressed against the glass. "I like your touch, Jay. Mmmmmmh, this feels good. Mmmmmmh." His sudden taking of control also turned her on. Now looking out of the window at the people and cars down below, it was adding to her euphoric stimulation, accompanied by his fast-moving fingers and intimate love bites. Lost in the moment of pleasure, she even started gyrating her hip as his fingers slid in and out. "Mmmmmmh, ooooh, this is so good, Jay," she moaned, feeling her body reacting with a sensation that was like feathers caressing her pearl and flesh. Her legs tightened, her hips halted in place, as the powerful surging streamed through her body ready to escape. She let it flow over his fingertips, as her mouth opened, breathing heavily, steaming up the window in front of her. He removed his fingers and turned her around, placing a kiss on her lips, before raising his fingers up to enjoy a taste of her pleasure. Then he removed her pants slowly, taking them down to her ankles. "Jay, what if Melanie comes in here and sees us like this?"

"She won't. She's on her computer with her boyfriend. Now let me take control of this, pleasing my lady." She didn't resist his touch as he removed her pants. He remained on one knee, taking her left leg over his right shoulder, kissing up her thigh before raising her entire body off the floor, allowing her right leg to go over her shoulder. She'd never had this happen to her before. His fingers and tongue touching and thrusting in and out of her body as she was up against the window, looking out over her shoulder, enjoying his tongue play and view, turned on by the feeling of falling accompanied with his oral magic.

"Aaaah, aaaaah, Jay, aaaaah, mmmmmmh, mmmmh," she moaned as her legs clenched, trying to brace for this orgasmic wave that was racing through her body. This was more intense than the first. Her heart, mind, and body were deeply into this erotic sensation that was soaring through her body. "Aaaaah, Aaaaah, ooooooh, Jay, ooooooooh, aaaaaaah." Her stomach was tightening, and her breathing was picking up. At the same time, he was lowering her body, he slowed his oral, allowing her flow to erupt. Her back was against the window, eyes closed, still breathing heavy. He let her legs down, coming up to her. She opened her eyes, looking at his glossy lips. "I love this version of you," she said wiping his lips before placing a kiss on them. "Let's take this show into the bedroom. There's more I want to show you," he said, leading the way. Once in the bedroom, each of them removed their clothing, appreciating the art of each other's flesh. He pulled the covers back, allowing her to get under them first. He followed, allowing his warm, firm flesh to embrace hers. "I'm going to make this very special," he said, kissing her breast, down to her side, back up before sliding on top of her and looking into her eyes. She extended her hand, taking his fully erect manhood that was pulsating into her grasp as she's guided it into her place of passion. His heart was racing, wanting to please her in every way, at the same time wanting it to be special for her. "You feel good, Danelle," he said, pressing deeply and slowly into her body, that was already sensitive and stimulated from his fingers and oral magic. With each deep stroke side to side, in and out, Jay could feel his heart racing and that long awaited sensation bouncing around inside, making his movement more intense. "I want to love you forever, Danelle. I love the way this feels."

His words stimulated her heart and body, making her moans intense. "Aaaaaaah, aaaaaaah, Jay, baby, aaaaaaah, aaaaaaah, aaaaah. I love you, too, mmmmh, mmmmmmh." Jay started going faster and deeper, feeling that uncontrollable eruption coming. At the same time, Danelle's body was releasing with powerful, intense pleasure. "Ooooh, ooooh God, Jay, don't move. Oooooh, mmmmmmh, mmmmm." Her moans were intense and shifted to heavy breathing as multiple orgasms were streaming through her body. This level of intensity was euphoric.

Moments later, he rolled to the side of her, to retrieve something from the side of the bed, before coming back under the covers with her. He also had his phone in hand, accessing a low light. "Here's the best part of how this night is going to end," he said, bringing a hunter-green case into view, lined with 24-karat-gold words that reads: "Harry Winston of Beverly Hills." She'd heard of this name before associated with celebrities and award shows. Her heart was fluttering as he opened the jewelry box revealing a brilliant solitary six-carat flawless diamond, custom designed and set in white gold. Her eyes filled with love, sparkling as much as the diamond. "I know this is untraditional, lying here in bed with a really sexy woman who has captured my attention in every way, but, Danelle, you're the woman I want to love and be loved by for the rest of my life. I want to be the one you wake up to each day, knowing you made the best decision in your life. So will you marry me, so I can be the luckiest man alive?"

"Yes, I will marry you. Yes, I will love and appreciate you and all you do for me and your love," she said, allowing him to slide the ring on. Her heart beat with love for him, just as his heart was for her. "No matter where I am or where you are, this ring is a true representation of our love," he said, placing a kiss on her lips that ignited another round of love and passion, which was even more special and meaningful, with this new future of love.

Chapter Twenty-Five

The morning hours came quick, after a long night of intimate lovemaking. Jay was already out of bed, securing calls for today's press release of his big reveal. Once he was done, he came back into the room, looking on at Danelle's flawless nude body, sleeping peacefully. His future wife, he was thinking with a smile on his face, ready to share his love story with the world. He came over to her bedside, placing a kiss on her cheek, then her lips, slowly awakening her. Her eyes opened slowly. "It's time to start our day, my love. I want the world to know I'm alive, well, and in love with this beautiful creature lying here in bed," he said, making her heart and face smile.

At the same time, she looked at her sparkling ring. "You want me to make you breakfast, babe?" she asked.

"We have a chef for that. I will, however, take you up on this one day, giving you a chance to spoil me with your love in the kitchen," he responded. "By the time you get out of the shower, the chef will have breakfast for you. Oh, one more thing, I kept Melanie from going to school this morning because once we go public, she'll need security, unless we send her to private school or home school."

"She loves her friends at school now, so we'll have to figure out something to keep her happy and safe too," Danelle responded as she made her way into the bathroom to shower. He appreciated the view from behind, as well as the thoughts of loving her body forever. Jay called up his best friend, Anthony. He picked up on the second ring.

"Well if it isn't the boss in disguise. How the hell are you, my friend?" Anthony asked. Aubry was at his side on the couch wondering who he was talking about.

"It's time, my friend. I called the press to the top of the building, since I'll be leaving the country on vacation with my new fiancé to South Africa. I want you to invite Aubry and have her reach out to Kim. She deserves to be here today."

"What time?"

"Eleven this morning. I'm on a tight schedule, so make sure everything is in line."

"It will be. I've been waiting for this for years," he said, glad he didn't have to continue lying in interviews about his whereabouts.

After the call, Jay made his way out to the chef who was sitting with Melanie as she was eating, texting, and talking. "Chef, you can make the usual for Danelle," Jay said. She obliged, turning around to prepare her food. "Now, Melanie, this school situation, I want what's best for you. If you want to stay there, we can provide security, since there will be media hounds always asking questions, along with the competition pressuring you for info."

Melanie didn't want to leave her school with all of her friends there, even if she could stay in contact with them through social media. "I want to stay there with my friends," she said. Her main interest was the boy she'd been talking to.

"I'll make your mother aware of this."

"Of what?" Danelle said, coming into the room dressed sexy with her long legs in her D & G jeans, fit snug against her flesh, flowing over her curves. The light blue Michael Kors top lay on her breasts for his visual appreciation to unwrap later on.

"About school, Mom. I don't want to leave. I have friends there," Melanie responded.

"You say this for now. However, when you do decide to change your mind, Mel, we're with you on it," Danelle responded lovingly, still on an emotional and physical high from last night's intimate session.

Melanie looked on at her mom, wondering why she was so easygoing. Then she noticed the sparkling ring. "Wow, that is nice, Mom. You did a good job with that, Jay," Melanie said, taking her phone and snapping a picture of her mom's ring.

"He loves and cares about us, Mel," Danelle responded as the chef came up and handed her the breakfast.

"Congratulations on such a beautiful diamond engagement ring," Shailynn said.

"Thank you," Danelle responded before eating her food.

Once she was done with her food, Jay was ready to get the day started with the interview and press. "You ladies ready to enter my world of media spotlight?"

"As ready as we'll ever be," Danelle responded, coming over to his side and placing her soft hands on his arm as he led the way. Once inside of the elevator, he removed a key card with a special clearance program in it. He scanned the card, and a female automated voice came over the speaker. "Good morning, Mr. Michaels. This elevator will be taking you and your guest to the helipad. Is there any future request for your travels today?"

"Just make sure all of my arrangements for this trip are in line with no mishaps, please. One more thing: make sure there are gummy bears before takeoff," he said, knowing they were one of Melanie's favorite candies.

Once they were at the rooftop, the doors opened to the view of his custom eight-passenger helicopter that was outfitted with lavish amenities and comfort. It was painted a custom dark red with gray panels, and the back windows were tinted, allowing for pregame privacy. The interior was outfitted with a mini bar, TVs, a sound system, and more, that were all appreciated in the custom quiet cabin, canceling out all exterior sound from the chopper blades. It didn't take long for the media outlets to follow. CNN, HLN, FOX News, and even online bloggers were invited to get their first glimpse and interview of James Michaels, the CEO of AmeriLink, who'd been out of sight for eight years. Tony also came up to his good friend with Aubry at his side, who was looking on at Danelle, trying to pull it all together, since she didn't recognize this sexy man she was with.

"Anthony, my friend, it's good to see you without acting like we don't know one another," James said before looking over at Aubry, who had her eye on him. "I take it he didn't tell you on the way over here?"

"What are you supposed to tell me, Anthony?" Aubry said, feeling left out.

"Aubry, this is Jay, Fuzzy Beard. His real name is James Michaels, the CEO of AmeriLink, my now fiancé," Danelle said.

Right then Aubry's jaw dropped open, trying to visually process it all, since this sexy man looked nothing like Fuzzy Beard. Plus, the ring on her best friend's finger. "So, you're telling me that this sexy man right here is Jay like the letter J?" Aubry asked.

"Yes, it's me, licky lips," James said in his Jay tone of voice, making Aubry burst into laughter, still shocked by this whole thing.

"You two have been hiding this freaky secret relationship from me and Kim?" Aubry asked, looking at her ring. "Damn, you even got engaged, you sneaky bitch," Aubry said, shaking her head with a smile, appreciating her ring and newfound love.

Kim stood quiet, looking on at them, wishing she, too, had found a love like theirs.

"So no more Fuzzy Beard?" Aubry asked.

He and Danelle shook their heads no.

"You two deserve this, Jay," Kim said, knowing her best friend and seeing James for the person he really was out of character.

Interrupting their little talk, his assistant Alexi came over. "Mr. Michaels, they're ready for you," she said.

The media outlets formed a half circle around him, his friends, and his future wife as he began to speak, making the world aware of his existence as well his newfound love. He also held Melanie's hand, which sparked questions about whether she was his daughter. "AmeriLink will continue to grow with new technology, expanding our brand. Outside of that, I'm going to take some time with my fiancée and future wife, Danelle Dupri, who is the real reason I'm standing before you today. Her love is worth me sharing with the world," he said, looking over at her radiant smile and glowing eyes that were filled with love. He couldn't resist placing a kiss on her lips, to display to the world this wasn't an artifice; it was the real thing.

"Mr. Michaels, so the rumors of your company being bought by the Russians aren't true?"

"This company, as long as my best friend and I are alive, will never be sold."

"Mr. Michaels, the hack into your company has affected your stocks overnight. Can you reassure your shareholders that things will be looking up from this point?"

"My presence alone will make the stocks excel too all-new high. As for the hack, nothing came of it, because of the fail safe I created. I also have smart, hard-working people like these ladies here," he said, turning to the pilot and signaling him to start the chopper. Then he turned back to his best friend. "Tony, I'll be back in a week. I'm going to live a little with my fiancée and family. Give Kim a manager position. It's the least we can do for her after the embarrassment yesterday. With that comes a bonus for her."

"I'll secure that. Enjoy your trip," Tony said. Jay and Danelle hugged their friends before getting into the chopper. Once the doors closed, the media focused their cameras on the chopper. Melanie was excited, never being in a helicopter before. The media watched the luxury chopper lift off, each of them filling in the blanks to this billionaire's return with a new love interest. As Melanie stared out at the buildings and houses below, Danelle placed intimate kisses on James's lips, loving the feeling he gave her. As they were heading to the airport where his private G4 jet was with two million in custom features, across town, Amber Michelle along with Trevor, who went back to her, were watching the news feed on their cell phones of this billionaire who came out of hiding when he found his true love. Trevor saw how he really messed up with her. Now she was gone forever, no looking back. Amber Michelle, as a woman, was loving the fairy-tale love story that was unfolding on every news network and blog. She was also wishing she was the one with this billionaire mogul.

"He's cute, rich, and smart. She landed a good one," Amber said , caressing him. "Don't worry, Trevor, we have each other the way we always wanted," she said, not realizing her words were stinging deep inside of him as he's felt the loss of a true once in a lifetime love.

Chapter Twenty-Six

Six months after the unexpected proposal and making a public appearance, James Michaels along with Danelle were set to get married today. Aubry was the maid of honor, ready to support her best friend, since she was there for her wedding two months ago, making her Mrs. West. Kim, after moving up in the company, swore off the men online. However, she did find someone by chance—a gentleman she bumped into at the grocery store. He was a well groomed Mercedes Benz dealer named George Rolstein, with a close shaven beard, a clean bald head, and thick eyebrows. His personality and confidence lured her in, giving her the comfort, she'd yearned for in his six-foot-two frame, being the protector of her heart and body. He was also present today as her plus one.

Danelle, Kim, and Aubry were in the large room of the forty thousand-square-foot mansion owned by James. He had purchased it because Danelle said she thought it would be a good place to have a wedding. This way she could have her wedding and memories of this place forever. The colors of the wedding were white with gold and diamonds for the ladies. The best man was already boasting a diamond encrusted Franck Mueller.

"I never thought this day would come," Danelle said, staring into the floor-to-ceiling mirror, looking on at herself in this picturesque custom designed Versace dress, made by Donatella and her staff. She, too, was present to appreciate her art in the dress as well as the love story unfolding. "Look at me ready to walk down the aisle with the man I truly love that finally loves me the same."

"You deserve it after all you've been through. None of us would have expected it to be Jay like the letter J, who turned out to be your sexy knight in shining armor, looking like a *GQ* model," Aubry said as they all laughed.

"Kim, Aubry, I love you guys. I'm so glad you're here to share this special day. It means the world to me."

"I wouldn't miss this for anything," Kim said, giving her a hug. "Now let's take shots, before you run off forever, married and traveling the world."

"Shots for nerves, love, and making memories," Aubry said, raising her glass and toasting. After the shots, they left Danelle to her stylist and makeup crew to put on their finishing touches.

She was now flawless looking in her veil, draped in diamonds, along with her diamond Tiffany bracelet, watch, and earrings, all accompanying her six-carat diamond engagement ring. She was looking like a true princess, a leading lady in her unfolding love story.

"Ms. Dupri, they're ready when you are," the wedding planner said, wanting to keep everything on track with all of the celebrities and billionaire elites present. They also had a platinum recording artist who was going to start as soon as she was ready.

"I'm ready as I'll ever be to love this man forever," Danelle said, smiling, feeling the butterflies of love.

"Bride to be is on the move," the wedding planner radioed to all of her assistants so everything could go as planned. The celebrity singer started singing as she started out. To her surprise, it was her favorite singer, John Legend, performing a song that defined what love is, a song that described how she felt for James. Danelle walked down the rose-laced steps leading down the aisle. The guest all looked on at her stunning beauty illuminated by love. Each step was gracefully taken for and toward her true love. Her diamonds sparkled under the sun that was accompanying the mood. James, for the first time in twenty-four hours, was seeing his future wife approaching. Ms. Michaels, his mother, was also present, looking youthful with a smile seeing her future daughter-in-law coming down the aisle. James was smiling as he watched her come down. Tony nudged James, excited too.

"This is it, my boy. You ready for this life?" Tony asked.

"She's the only one for me, Tony," he responded. Danelle made it past the front row, seeing her mother-in-law as well as her friends. She came up standing in front of James, who was looking nervous but in love with this woman.

The wedding preacher started the ceremony before allowing the two of them to recite their own vows full of love and promises each of them would keep until their dying breath. "I now pronounce you Mr. and Mrs. Michaels. You may kiss your bride." James and Danelle pulled one another into a passionate loving kiss, that had even more meaning than the others they'd shared. This was her first official kiss as Mrs. Michaels. As they were kissing, clapping and crying could be heard, full of love and joy, as the celebrity singer started off with another song.

James pulled back from the kiss, looking on at his new bride. "I thought I was the only one that took a shot before the wedding," he said, tasting the apple Cîroc on her tongue.

"It was Aubry's idea," she responded, blaming her friend and turning to look over at Aubry with a smile. James took her hand and walked back down the aisle toward the mansion, coming alive emotionally, feeling the love from Danelle. Melanie was also smiling and crying, happy for her mother, looking on at her glowing with happiness.

"I love you, Mrs. Michaels," he said, allowing the magic of this moment to permeate through his body. "Most couples reached their climax at this point of life and love. Not you and I. This is our beginning," he said, making her light up with love inside and out.

"I love you, too, Jay like the letter J," she said, being truthful and funny, since she fell for him and his wise words as he was at the office, not as the billionaire that would attract most women. Hearing her say this allowed him to know he didn't need AmeriLink's dating site to tell him he had made the right choice with her, because when love happens, the heart will take over guiding you to your happy ending.

To order books, please fill out the order form below:

To order films please go to www.good2gofilms.com

Name:____
Address:____
City:______________State:________Zip Code: ____________
Phone:____
Email:____
Method of Payment: Check VISA MASTERCARD
Credit Card#:____
Name as it appears on card: ________________________________
Signature: ____

Item Name	Price	Qty	Amount
48 Hours to Die – Silk White	$14.99		
A Hustler's Dream – Ernest Morris	$14.99		
A Hustler's Dream 2 – Ernest Morris	$14.99		
A Thug's Devotion – J. L. Rose and J. M. McMillon	$14.99		
All Eyes on Tommy Gunz – Warren Holloway	$14.99		
Black Reign – Ernest Morris	$14.99		
Bloody Mayhem Down South – Trayvon Jackson	$14.99		
Bloody Mayhem Down South 2 – Trayvon Jackson	$14.99		
Business Is Business – Silk White	$14.99		
Business Is Business 2 – Silk White	$14.99		
Business Is Business 3 – Silk White	$14.99		
Cash In Cash Out – Assa Raymond Baker	$14.99		
Cash In Cash Out 2 – Assa Raymond Baker	$14.99		
Childhood Sweethearts – Jacob Spears	$14.99		
Childhood Sweethearts 2 – Jacob Spears	$14.99		
Childhood Sweethearts 3 – Jacob Spears	$14.99		
Childhood Sweethearts 4 – Jacob Spears	$14.99		
Connected To The Plug – Dwan Marquis Williams	$14.99		
Connected To The Plug 2 – Dwan Marquis Williams	$14.99		
Connected To The Plug 3 – Dwan Williams	$14.99		
Cost of Betrayal – W.C. Holloway	$14.99		
Cost of Betrayal 2 – W.C. Holloway	$14.99		
Deadly Reunion – Ernest Morris	$14.99		
Dream's Life – Assa Raymond Baker	$14.99		
Finding Her Love – Warren C. Holloway	$14.99		
Flipping Numbers – Ernest Morris	$14.99		
Flipping Numbers 2 – Ernest Morris	$14.99		

Forbidden Pleasure – Ernest Morris	$14.99		
He Loves Me, He Loves You Not – Mychea	$14.99		
He Loves Me, He Loves You Not 2 – Mychea	$14.99		
He Loves Me, He Loves You Not 3 – Mychea	$14.99		
He Loves Me, He Loves You Not 4 – Mychea	$14.99		
He Loves Me, He Loves You Not 5 – Mychea	$14.99		
Killing Signs – Ernest Morris	$14.99		
Killing Signs 2 – Ernest Morris	$14.99		
Kings of the Block – Dwan Willams	$14.99		
Kings of the Block 2 – Dwan Willams	$14.99		
Lord of My Land – Jay Morrison	$14.99		
Lost and Turned Out – Ernest Morris	$14.99		
Love & Dedication – W.C. Holloway	$14.99		
Love Hates Violence – De'Wayne Maris	$14.99		
Love Hates Violence 2 – De'Wayne Maris	$14.99		
Love Hates Violence 3 – De'Wayne Maris	$14.99		
Love Hates Violence 4 – De'Wayne Maris	$14.99		
Married To Da Streets – Silk White	$14.99		
M.E.R.C. – Make Every Rep Count Health and Fitness	$14.99		
Mercenary In Love – J.L. Rose & J.L. Turner	$14.99		
Money Make Me Cum – Ernest Morris	$14.99		
My Besties – Asia Hill	$14.99		
My Besties 2 – Asia Hill	$14.99		
My Besties 3 – Asia Hill	$14.99		
My Besties 4 – Asia Hill	$14.99		
My Boyfriend's Wife – Mychea	$14.99		
My Boyfriend's Wife 2 – Mychea	$14.99		
My Brothers Envy – J. L. Rose	$14.99		
My Brothers Envy 2 – J. L. Rose	$14.99		
Naughty Housewives – Ernest Morris	$14.99		
Naughty Housewives 2 – Ernest Morris	$14.99		
Naughty Housewives 3 – Ernest Morris	$14.99		
Naughty Housewives 4 – Ernest Morris	$14.99		
Never Be The Same – Silk White	$14.99		
Scarred Faces – Assa Raymond Baker	$14.99		

Scarred Knuckles – Assa Raymond Baker	$14.99		
Secrets in the Dark – Ernest Morris	$14.99		
Secrets in the Dark 2 – Ernest Morris	$14.99		
Shades of Revenge – Assa Raymond Baker	$14.99		
Slumped – Jason Brent	$14.99		
Someone's Gonna Get It – Mychea	$14.99		
Stranded – Silk White	$14.99		
Supreme & Justice – Ernest Morris	$14.99		
Supreme & Justice 2 – Ernest Morris	$14.99		
Supreme & Justice 3 – Ernest Morris	$14.99		
Tears of a Hustler – Silk White	$14.99		
Tears of a Hustler 2 – Silk White	$14.99		
Tears of a Hustler 3 – Silk White	$14.99		
Tears of a Hustler 4 – Silk White	$14.99		
Tears of a Hustler 5 – Silk White	$14.99		
Tears of a Hustler 6 – Silk White	$14.99		
The Betrayal Within – Ernest Morris	$14.99		
The Last Love Letter – Warren Holloway	$14.99		
The Last Love Letter 2 – Warren Holloway	$14.99		
The Panty Ripper – Reality Way	$14.99		
The Panty Ripper 3 – Reality Way	$14.99		
The Solution – Jay Morrison	$14.99		
The Teflon Queen – Silk White	$14.99		
The Teflon Queen 2 – Silk White	$14.99		
The Teflon Queen 3 – Silk White	$14.99		
The Teflon Queen 4 – Silk White	$14.99		
The Teflon Queen 5 – Silk White	$14.99		
The Teflon Queen 6 – Silk White	$14.99		
The Vacation – Silk White	$14.99		
The Webpage Murder – Ernest Morris	$14.99		
The Webpage Murder 2 – Ernest Morris	$14.99		
Tied To A Boss – J.L. Rose	$14.99		
Tied To A Boss 2 – J.L. Rose	$14.99		
Tied To A Boss 3 – J.L. Rose	$14.99		
Tied To A Boss 4 – J.L. Rose	$14.99		
Tied To A Boss 5 – J.L. Rose	$14.99		

Time Is Money – Silk White	$14.99		
Tomorrow's Not Promised – Robert Torres	$14.99		
Tomorrow's Not Promised 2 – Robert Torres	$14.99		
Two Mask One Heart – Jacob Spears and Trayvon Jackson	$14.99		
Two Mask One Heart 2 – Jacob Spears and Trayvon Jackson	$14.99		
Two Mask One Heart 3 – Jacob Spears and Trayvon Jackson	$14.99		
When Love Happens – Warren Holloway	$14.99		
Wife – Assa Ray Baker & Raneissa Baker	$14.99		
Wife 2 – Assa Ray Baker & Raneissa Baker	$14.99		
Wrong Place Wrong Time – Silk White	$14.99		
Young Goonz – Reality Way	$14.99		
Subtotal:			
Tax:			
Shipping (Free) U.S. Media Mail:			
Total:			

Make Checks Payable to Good2Go Publishing, 7311 W Glass Lane, Laveen, AZ 85339

CPSIA information can be obtained
at www.ICGtesting.com
Printed in the USA
BVHW041826210322
632026BV00016B/242